BOOK TWO

Danny,

  keep working
hard my friend!

    Enjoy,

A coprid they carved me in agate and gold; on a Pharaoh's neck
I lay. They put us away in a cave of old, and I carry
a text of The Book of the Dead *as I roll my ball of clay.*

—"THE SCARAB," A POEM BY IVAN SWIFT PUBLISHED
IN THE *SCARAB* OCTOBER 1914 ISSUE

Text copyright © 2017 William Meyer
Interior illustrations copyright © 2017 William Meyer

Cover illustration by Gerald Kelley

Sleeping Bear Press™

2395 South Huron Parkway, Suite 200, Ann Arbor, MI 48104
www.sleepingbearpress.com
© Sleeping Bear Press

Printed and bound in the United States.
10 9 8 7 6 5 4 3 2 1

Library of Congress Cataloging-in-Publication Data
Names: Meyer, William, 1979- author.
Title: The search for the lost prophecy / William Meyer.
Description: Ann Arbor, MI : Sleeping Bear Press, [2017]
Series: Horace j. Edwards and the Time Keepers ;
book two | Summary: Horace and his friends
travel back in time to 1920s Detroit, where they learn that the
mystical Benben Stone is being stored in present-day Niles, Michigan, and
Horace is tasked with keeping the sacred stone safe. Includes historical note.
Identifiers: LCCN 2017016985 | ISBN 9781585369829
Subjects: | CYAC: Time travel--Fiction. | Prophecies--Fiction.
Supernatural--Fiction. | Secret societies--Fiction. | Detroit
(Mich.)--History--20th century--Fiction.
Classification: LCC PZ7.1.M5 Sb 2017 | DDC [Fic]--dc23
LC record available at https://lccn.loc.gov/2017016985

To Liam, the next in a long line of Keepers
—Bill

HORACE j. EDWARDS *and the* TIME KEEPERS

the
search for the
Lost prophecy

BOOK TWO

wiLLiam meyer

PUBLISHED BY SLEEPING BEAR PRESS

chapter one

*T*he rustling sound of leaves and swaying branches filled the air. Horace was on the front porch of his house, but he couldn't tell if it was morning or night; everything was cast in a bluish-gray light.

He walked down the steps and across the front sidewalk. Was it Halloween already? *he wondered to himself. But where were all the trick-or-treaters? The street was empty.*

And where was his costume? *Horace was wearing his pajamas.*

On the other side of the street a tall iron fence stretched out in both directions. At the center was an arched gateway. Next to the gate were two redheaded boys, each in matching plaid shirts. *They looked identical, except one was a few inches taller, and maybe a few years older than the other one.*

The boys waved at Horace to follow them, and then they disappeared through the gate into a swirling fog.

Horace slowly walked across the empty street and cautiously approached the entrance. He pushed the iron gate open. He could see a dark field beyond and a gravel path that meandered into it.

One of the redheaded boys reappeared next to Horace's side. "There is a great secret in this town. A secret for you to discover." The boy waved and disappeared again.

Horace realized that he was now standing on the gravel path. He began to walk the strange winding trail. The gravel seemed to crunch like exploding popcorn under the weight of his feet. As he walked along, he noticed that several headstones had now appeared in the once-empty field. Horace realized this was a cemetery, and continued his journey.

Now he could see the two boys standing side by side at the end of the path, waving vigorously. "Hurry, hurry. Someone else seeks the prophecy!" the younger boy yelled, and then ran toward a crypt nestled into the side of a small sloping hill.

The path guided Horace directly to the mysterious tomb. A single step led to a marble landing. The tomb's entrance was lined with fine marble, and two urns containing dried flowers framed the doorway. Above the doorway was a single word, BEESON.

Now the two boys stood at the entrance.

They beckoned Horace to follow before disappearing.

Horace walked up the step and stood on the landing. He stared at the thick wooden doors. On each was a large, cast-iron loop handle. Horace lifted the handle on the right door and began to pull. Slowly but steadily it opened. His heart raced as he anticipated what could be inside.

And then a blinding light woke him.

chapter two

The next day Horace was consumed by thoughts of his dream. It was the end of the weekend, and as he finished up his homework, he couldn't stop thinking of the strange images and what they might mean. Who were the boys? What was the prophecy they mentioned? And where was this mysterious tomb?

It wasn't until much later in the afternoon, while at his grandparents' farm, that Horace finally had the time to think about the dream. The family had returned to the farm to clean and move out the last of his grandparents' belongings. After an hour of helping his sisters roll up oriental carpets, vacuum the wood floors, and move boxes of old clothes and framed photos up from the basement into the front hall, Horace wandered outside for a little break. As soon as he stepped out into the open field behind the farmhouse, Shadow swooped down and brushed Horace's tangled hair with a wing before soaring back up in the air.

Over the weeks since his adventures through the sycamore tree, Horace had grown ever closer to the beautiful falcon. She circled around in the blue fall sky and then dove toward the ground, this time brushing the back of his neck with her soft tail feathers. Horace let out a loud laugh as she tickled his skin.

Shadow almost never left his side anymore. At night she kept watch from a perch on his bedroom windowsill and then followed him each morning as he rode his bike to school. During lunch she'd stare watchfully from the chain-link fence across the field while he played with his friends. Even in the afternoon, as he sat in class with the other sixth-graders listening to Mr. Petrie's endless lectures, outside she circled overhead, diligently waiting for the school bell to ring and Horace to emerge for the afternoon. The other kids had also grown accustomed to her presence—everyone except for Seth. The scars on his forearm from her attack a month earlier were still raw. And while he had been a great ally when they had time-traveled to Egypt, immediately upon their return to school, Seth had reverted to his old bullying ways.

This afternoon was no different. Shadow spiraled and twisted in the air while Horace walked across the open field. The rest of the family was inside the farmhouse while Horace wandered around. He was happy to have a little fresh air to make sense of the strange dream from the night before and take inventory of all he'd experienced since his grandfather's death. The painful memory of that event always resurfaced when he returned to the farm.

The circumstances surrounding his grandfather's death had sent Horace on a desperate scavenger hunt for answers. But the hunt had only revealed more secrets, which even now he struggled to make sense of, particularly in light of the strange dream.

Weeks before, Horace had uncovered a hidden doorway in his grandfather's office that led to a tunnel under the farm. The tunnel connected the house with an old syca-more tree in the backyard. When Horace had first found the tunnel, he thought he had discovered a forgotten remnant of the Underground Railroad. However, the intended use of the tunnel, which ended just feet from the sycamore tree, was not at all connected to this well-known chapter in Nile's history. It was tied to an even greater and older secret. Hidden within the bark of the tree was a doorway to Ancient Egypt. The discovery of this portal and the scarab beetle that unlocked it had changed Horace's life.

The scarab beetle was a small stone amulet, which had proven to be more than just an ancient souvenir dating back to Egypt. It was also a powerful key that unlocked a portal across time. The beetle connected Horace to his grandfather and an order of guardians known as the Keepers of Time. But this had also raised questions for Horace. What did it truly mean to be a Keeper of Time? How far back did the Order stretch? Were there any other Keepers today or in Niles?

As Horace wandered around the field, kicking at piles of leaves that had accumulated, other questions began to surface. Were there more portals to be discovered, places besides Egypt to explore, and other secrets of the Time Keepers to be revealed? Who were the Time Keepers? What did it mean to be part of the Order? What was his role? It was this growing list of questions that kept Horace awake most nights, staring at the model airplanes dangling from his ceiling.

He turned his attention back to Shadow. "Where do you think Herman went?" he asked as Shadow circled overhead. "Did he go back to Egypt?" Herman was the enigmatic figure who had given Horace the beetle, showing up at his house unannounced the first week of school.

Shadow let out a shrill cry and swooped up toward the sky.

As a friend of his grandfather's and a mentor to Horace, Herman had introduced Horace into the secrets of the Order, answering many of his initial questions. But after the last adventure through the portal and a climactic battle at the farm, Herman had disappeared. What made his disappearance even more upsetting was the fact that he had also taken with him the Benben Stone, a powerful relic that Horace had helped to recover. Herman had refused to tell Horace where he was taking it, making Horace feel both helpless and frustrated. He desperately wanted to make his grandfather proud and fulfill his legacy as a Keeper, but Herman had hinted that the boy had much to learn before he could be trusted to watch over the most prized artifact of the Order.

The Benben Stone was an ancient artifact that Horace and his friends had recovered from King Tut's uncle Smenk. The stone contained many great powers. One of those was its ability to possess memories, which could then be accessed by a Time Keeper using a scarab beetle. It was like a living library of historical knowledge that dated all the way back to Ancient Egypt. As far as Horace could tell, the purpose of the Order was to protect and guard the secrets of the ancient stone. As he stared up at the white clouds in the afternoon sky, he wondered what other powers this sacred object might possess.

Now Shadow dove down, landing on a lower branch of the sycamore tree a few feet from Horace. Her coal-black eyes stared intensely at the horizon.

Horace pulled the beetle out of his pocket and flipped it over in his hand. The beetle shimmered a dull blue light; a collection of hieroglyphics covered the flat surface of its belly.

"Do you think there might be other Keepers out there besides just Herman and me?" he asked Shadow.

A small squirrel ran across the field toward the farm-house, and Shadow dove from her perch, sending the tiny animal scurrying for cover. Shadow's speed, her beauty, and her power always amazed Horace. There were few creatures that seemed to move through the air so gracefully but also with such power. It was no wonder that one of the most powerful Egyptian gods was a falconlike winged creature. A god who just so happened to also be Horace's namesake, as well as one of the secret symbols he'd seen used by the Order to distinguish their members.

Thinking of Egypt sparked more questions in Horace's mind. Was Tut okay? Was he king of Egypt now? And married? What had happened to Amarna, the city his father had built? Time moved more quickly on the other side of the portal, and it had been almost two weeks since he'd traveled there on his last adventure.

Shadow swooped upward and returned to her perch on the tree. Horace wondered if maybe he could risk a little peek and see how things were going.

"What do you think, Shadow? Should we check it out and see what's been happening?"

The bird let out an even louder squawk, which Horace was unable to decipher as either a yes or a no.

His heart started to beat rapidly as he thought about going through the portal.

He twirled the beetle over in his hand and made up his mind. Despite Herman's warnings, Horace *was* going to visit Ancient Egypt. If Herman wasn't going to show up to answer his questions, Horace would just have to go looking for answers himself.

He gazed down at the beetle in his palm. At various times throughout his adventures the beetle had emitted a blue light whenever Horace was near the portal. But now it appeared lifeless and cold to the touch.

Horace guessed that he probably wasn't close enough to the tree portal to engage the magic. *It would soon come to life,* he told himself. *I just need to get closer.*

Horace took a quick glance at the farmhouse to make sure no one was looking. He could see the silhouettes of his two sisters in the windowpanes of the second-floor office. Soon they'd be expecting him to return and help them finish packing his grandparents' stuff.

He turned toward the tree and walked over to the widest part of the trunk, a spot where a small notch marked the keyhole to the portal. *It'll only take a moment. I'll be back before anyone knows I'm gone.*

As Horace approached, he couldn't help but remember the first time he'd discovered the portal and the inescapable pull he'd felt from the beetle. It was so strong that the stone literally flew out of his hand to find its way to the bark. Now, though, there was no magnetic draw.

He passed under the canopy of the branches and realized that something was wrong. It wasn't the distance from the tree anymore; he was just an arm's length away. But the beetle emitted no light, and there was no sensation of it trying to pull away from his hand, not even a twinge on his skin.

Horace stepped closer. Then he felt as though his heart dropped to the ground, and his eyes widened in horror. He blinked, wondering if what he was seeing was real or his imagination. He rubbed the palm of his free hand against the surface of the trunk to confirm it.

There in the bark of the sycamore tree, where Horace had once placed the beetle to open the portal to Egypt, a blackened X had been carved.

Horace gasped, and Shadow let out a shriek.

It looked like someone had intentionally sliced out the keyhole with a knife or some other type of sharp instrument.

He stared again in disbelief, rubbing his fingers against the rough surface. Hot flashes spread up Horace's back and down his arms. What was he going to do? The reality of what he was staring at began to sink in. The portal! It had been destroyed! This severed his connection to Egypt.

He looked down at the beetle. It was as lifeless as a stone from the gravel driveway. Someone had intentionally destroyed the keyhole. But who?

Horace started to breathe quickly. A panicky feeling

spread under his skin and around his lungs like a snake suffocating its prey. Beads of sweat appeared on his brow. He bit down on his bottom lip. How was he going to reach Tut or Herman? What did this mean? Who would have done such a thing?

CHAPTER THREE

"Horace!" his mother shouted from the screen door. "Horace, we need your help!"

He snapped around, startled by the intrusion.

"I'll be right there!" he answered in return.

She closed the door, and Horace returned his attention to the carving in the tree.

Just to make certain he was correct, he tried to slide the beetle into the mutilated bark. But there was no place for it to fit, and no spark of light or color—no magic.

His eyes widened, and his heart sank. The portal was inaccessible. "This isn't good," he said to Shadow. What was he going to do? He had always thought if he wanted to reconnect with Tut, he would just use the beetle and slip through the portal. But now that connection was lost.

He instinctively reached into his pocket to grab his phone but realized that was useless. There was no reception at the farm, and even if the phone did work, he didn't have Herman's number. Who knew if Herman even had a phone?

Shadow let out another loud shriek and dove off her branch, brushing Horace's right arm.

"I know, Shadow, we need to be on guard. Someone out there destroyed the portal. Someone might know about the Keepers," Horace said, his voice rising in distress.

"Horace!" his mom shouted again, this time from the upstairs window.

"I'm coming," he answered in a shaky voice.

A thousand thoughts ran through his mind. What was he going to do? He couldn't use the beetle, and he couldn't reach Herman by phone. But he had to tell Herman that the portal had been destroyed. But where was Herman?

Shadow shrieked loudly and sailed up into the afternoon sky.

"Horace!" one of his sisters now shouted. "We don't have all day!"

"I'm coming!" Horace slipped the beetle into his pocket and quickly ran across to the screen door at the back of the house. The hinges opened with a loud whine.

As he entered the kitchen he let out a sneeze, wiping the end of his nose with his sleeve. The house had taken on a musty smell since his grandfather's death and his grandmother's departure to a nursing home. The kitchen was almost completely empty except for the cable wires that had once been connected to the television. Even the living room had been cleared of all furniture, including the couch where Horace had sat only a month earlier with his grandma when she had first hinted at the existence of the portal.

"Hurry up, Horace. We need your help upstairs!" Lilly, his older sister, called. "We're in Grandpa's office."

Lilly was one of Horace's two older sisters. Sara was the other. They both loved to harass him.

The front door was open, and now his mom and dad were hauling boxes at the foot of the steps out to his uncle's car in the driveway. While Horace and his friends had successfully thwarted his uncle's earlier efforts to sell the farm, it hadn't guaranteed the protection and safekeeping of the objects inside. His uncle George was now trying to make any money he could by selling the valuable antiques on eBay and donating the rest.

"Are you okay?" his mom asked as she lifted another box full of books from the steps.

Horace blinked, trying to hide any expression of worry and come up with a quick explanation for his behavior. "Yeah, I'm fine. I just have to finish my math homework when we get home."

"Don't worry about that now. You'll have plenty of time after dinner," his mom said with a smile. "Your sisters are upstairs and need a little help bringing down the last of your grandpa's stuff."

"Okay," Horace answered. The wooden steps at the front of the house groaned as he made his way to the second-floor landing. The photographs that once lined the walls were gone, and a constellation of nail holes marked the paint like the Milky Way stretching across the sky.

The bedrooms, like the living room, were also empty of both furniture and carpets. Dark rectangular blotches marked where oriental rugs had once covered the hardwood floors, and outlines of where pictures had hung stained the walls.

His grandfather's office was at the end of the hall. It stood empty except for three wall-mounted shelves holding some books and an old antique grandfather clock that leaned against one wall.

"No one can get this thing to move," said Sara, noticing the direction of Horace's gaze. "It's made of solid mahogany."

Horace nodded in agreement, but he knew there was more to the clock than its weight keeping it in place.

"What do you need help with?" he asked, changing the subject.

"Mom wants us to clear off the bookshelves. If you could take the boxes by the door down to Mom, that would be helpful," said Lilly.

Horace bent down and tried to pick up the nearest cardboard box. "This weighs a ton," he said as he struggled to lift it.

Sara walked over and removed some of the books from the top of the box and placed them on the floor. "Don't worry. Mom had trouble lifting them. You are just going to have to make a few extra trips."

Horace was able to more easily maneuver the lighter box now and headed down the hall. Lilly followed, also carrying a box of books. They made the trip two more times, until they had completely emptied the last of the shelves.

"That should do it," Sara said, picking up the remaining books scattered along the floor. "This is the last one."

It was by far the lightest of all the boxes, with only a handful of books resting at the bottom.

"We can finally get home, and I can call my friends," said Lilly, holding her phone high up in the air. "I hate coming out here. You can't get any reception. I probably have, like, a thousand text messages."

They returned back down the stairs, where a box of books still sat, waiting to be taken out to the car. Horace was about to pick it up, when his uncle appeared in the doorway.

Uncle George was a real estate agent. His picture was posted on several billboards and on most of the For Sale signs around Niles. Horace thought his uncle considered himself a local celebrity, but he never quite trusted the man. He particularly disliked his uncle's intense interest in selling the farm and trying to turn a quick profit off his grandparents' belongings.

"What were you doing in the back again, Horace? Didn't I tell you not to fool around? We finally got that mess of a shed cleaned up from those kids who were out here two weeks ago. I hope it wasn't your friends."

Horace felt his face turn bright red.

"Stop giving him such a hard time, George," his mom said as she joined them in the entryway. "He's not doing anything wrong." Horace's uncle gave him another suspicious glare and then headed out to his car.

Horace's mom turned to him. "Horace, can you go upstairs and double-check that all the lights are off and we got everything? I'll take this stuff out to the car." She lifted the box from the bottom step.

"Okay." He turned and skipped up the stairs two at

a time.

The second floor was now completely dark. He walked down the hall and peered into each of the bedrooms. All the lights were off except for one in the office that his sisters must have forgotten about.

Horace flipped the light switch on the wall to off and took one quick glance around the room. Out the window the silhouette of the sycamore tree stood at the edge of the field. He felt a twinge of pain.

He was about to turn away, when he noticed his sisters had missed a book. It was on the floor in the corner. The faded leather cover blended into the dark wood, making it hard to see. *I probably would have missed it too*, thought Horace, *except for the light from the window catching the metal lock on the cover.*

He walked over and picked up the book. With a strong exhale, Horace blew off the dust that had gathered along the edges of the leather binding. He turned the book over in his hand. A small brass lock kept the front and back covers tightly closed. He looked at the binding for a name or title, and he saw an unmistakable mark. A symbol pressed deeply into the leather and outlined in black ink. This wasn't some random symbol. It was the marking of the Keepers, the eye of Horus.

It wasn't until recently that Horace had learned that his middle initial, a lowercase j, wasn't just a sloppy mistake on his birth certificate; it was actually the eye of Horus, an ancient Egyptian symbol of protection. This symbol had also marked Horace as a member of the Keepers from birth.

Now he felt something move in his pocket. At first he wondered if Milton or Anna, his two best friends, were calling his phone. But then he remembered Lilly complaining about the lack of cell reception at the farm.

He reached down and realized it was the beetle. For the first time in weeks it was vibrating furiously. He pulled it out and held it up alongside the old leather book.

The beetle was alive again. And it had changed colors! The surface, which he had only known as a deep ocean blue, now glowed a brilliant mint green. Why had it changed color?

Suddenly all the fear, all the sadness, all the dread

he had felt earlier when he had touched the damaged tree turned into excitement. Seeing the green light, Horace was filled with hope. He wondered if this might mark the opening of a new portal and a new adventure.

chapter four

Horace was anxious to tell his friends about what he'd discovered at the farm. The destruction of the portal was probably the most serious thing that had happened since the death of his grandfather. But the next day at school, as Horace joined the rush of kids entering the front door, an elbow rubbed up against his arm. He turned his head and saw standing next to him, only inches away, Seth.

Seth had been his partner on a previous school project and an unexpected compatriot on Horace's adventure in Egypt. However, he was also the biggest bully in the school. Horace noticed that since their return from Egypt Seth had resumed his old ways.

Horace whispered over to Seth, "Tell me something. Did you go back to my grandparents' farm and mess around with the portal?"

Seth looked secretive but nervously started to fidget with his hands. "I haven't been back there since our trip."

Horace didn't need to ask more, as by chance Shadow let out a loud shriek from above.

The sight of the falcon melted away any bravado Seth might have tried to muster. "I promise I didn't go back there. I wouldn't touch that thing. I saw what was on the other side, and it almost killed me!" Seth pushed his way forward through the crowd and ran into the building.

Horace rubbed his brow, confused by the encounter. He hardly had a moment to process what Seth had just said when Anna, following close behind, asked, "What did Seth want?"

Horace leaned in, keeping his voice low. "I asked him if he knew anything about the portal."

"Of course he knows about the portal. What did he say?" Milton asked, suddenly joining the two of them. "Has he been back out there?"

"I don't think so." Horace scanned the thinning crowd to make sure no one overheard them. "But yesterday I was at the farm with my family, and I wandered out into the yard. I was thinking I might just take a peek through the portal to check on Tut."

"You went back to Egypt?" Milton's eyes widened. "How is he?"

"I never found out," answered Horace.

"What do you mean?" asked Anna, growing confused.

"The keyhole to the portal was destroyed. Someone had taken a knife or something and slashed an X across the spot where the beetle used to go."

Horace's two friends now stood there in wide-eyed shock.

"I was certain it must have been Seth. He was the only other person who knew about the portal, and I can imagine he probably owns a switchblade. But when I confronted him just now, he said he had nothing to do with it," Horace said, furrowing his brow.

"You believe him?" Milton asked doubtfully.

Horace scratched his head. "I don't know who to

believe. I wish Herman would return. Since his disappearance I feel like I'm just drowning in questions." The school bell rang deep within the building.

"It sounds like we need to keep a lookout. If it wasn't Seth who damaged that portal, then someone else must know about it," said Anna.

"But who?" asked Horace.

"I don't know, but I still don't trust Seth," added Milton. "I think we've got to tell Herman."

"I know," said Horace, "but how? The tree was our only link to the past. The last time we saw Herman he was going through the portal there with Tut and Meri. And now we have no way of getting back."

Anna shrugged. "Maybe there's another way."

"You mean another portal here in town we could use?" asked Horace.

The bell rang a second time. They were now the last three students standing outside the entrance.

"Guys, we'd better hurry or we're going to be late," said Milton, glancing at his watch.

"Maybe there is also another Keeper you can find who

will help," suggested Anna.

Horace had been wondering about the possibility that other Keepers existed in Niles, but Herman had given him no indication who or where they might be.

Mr. Witherspoon, the school principal, was now standing at the front entrance. "Let's go, you three."

"If the tree portal is really gone, then I think we should put our efforts into finding a new one," whispered Anna.

"Wait." Horace raised his index finger. "I think I know where we can go and maybe find an answer to *both* of your questions."

"Where?" asked Milton.

Horace shouted, "The Niles Museum!"

CHapteR five

The museum was located on Main Street, only a few minutes' ride from Horace's house. And he was quite familiar with the old building. His grandfather had worked there for years. Unfortunately, Anna had basketball practice on Monday and Tuesday, and Milton got stuck watching his sister on Wednesday. So it wasn't until Thursday after school when they were all able to meet at the museum.

Horace had spent most of the week thinking about what they might find at the museum. He hadn't been back there since his grandfather's death.

The museum was located in a three-story redbrick Victorian mansion known as the Chapin House. A single turret marked the entrance to the building, where the main collection of the museum was held. A carriage house, connected at the back of the house, served as a secondary exhibit hall and provided storage space. Horace wondered if there was a chance the museum might have something in its city history section on the third floor.

An old dilapidated fountain sat outside at the front of the building. The fountainhead was in the shape of a giant head with a gnarled beard. From the rust stains around the mouth, the fountain looked like it hadn't worked in years.

Horace was still thinking about the destruction of the portal and whether they'd actually find information about another Time Keeper at the museum as he rode his bike up the circular driveway.

Anna's waving stopped his thoughts as he slid his front tire into the bike rack. "You made it. What took so long?"

"Sorry," Horace answered sheepishly. "I had to come up with an excuse to tell my mom. She'd get suspicious if all of a sudden I started visiting museums on my own."

"Well, let's get going and see if we can find anything about the Order," said Anna.

"Or even the portals," Milton added.

"Or the beetle." Horace reached down and patted his pocket.

"There, look." Milton pointed at the sky. Above them circled a shape. "Shadow followed you over here. That's got to be a good sign."

Horace stared at the bird in the sky. She had been sporadically around all week, coming and going from his window ledge. He noticed that she had seemed particularly agitated since the discovery of the damaged portal.

"Let's go," said Milton. "I'm supposed to babysit my little sister again later." He led them in through the front door as Shadow landed on top of the old fountainhead, settling on one of the ears.

The imposing and well-maintained interior of the museum, as compared to its worn exterior, immediately struck Horace. On the first floor a dozen ornate stained-glass windows let in light, illuminating a beveled mirror that stretched the full length of the entrance hall and an extraordinary wood fireplace. There was also a commanding brass chandelier hanging in the entrance above their heads.

No sooner had they stepped inside the door than an overly enthusiastic voice greeted them. "Welcome, welcome, welcome! What do we have here? Three young historians interested in learning about our town's past?" From out behind a small doorway stepped a short, stocky man. "Let me introduce myself. My name is Mr. Franken, and I'm one of the curators of the museum," he said, an awkward smile on his face.

"That's weird. I thought my grandfather had introduced me to everyone at the museum, but I don't remember seeing this guy," Horace whispered to Anna.

"Well, there are probably lots of workers you haven't met," answered Anna.

But something about it didn't feel right. The museum was small and didn't have many staff members. *Why wouldn't Grandpa have introduced me to Mr. Franken?* thought Horace. He turned his attention back toward their odd guide.

Mr. Franken's tie and jacket seemed to be moving in opposite directions. He had a scar across his left cheek, and his squeaky voice reached a high pitch at the end of each sentence. But the most remarkable feature of the curator was his hair, a comb-over that spanned from one ear to the other. A thick oily gel pasted it down.

Mr. Franken didn't seem to notice the kids' conversation and continued with his prepared opening lecture. "I see you have taken a liking to the beautiful artwork carved on our entrance fireplace. These designs date back to the nineteenth century when Henry Austin Chapin first built the mansion in 1884. These often go unnoticed by many visitors, but they were very common in this Queen Anne–style house. May I show you the rest of the collection?"

Milton gave Horace a hard nudge with his elbow.

"We were just hoping to look around by ourselves," Horace explained.

"Oh, no need for that!" answered Mr. Franken enthusiastically. "My next group won't be here for another half an hour. I can give you a private tour. You can't beat that!"

"Ummmm," Horace replied awkwardly. "Okay."

"What?" said Milton under his breath. "This is going to take forever."

"Excellent," said Mr. Franken. "Come with me."

"What's wrong with this guy? He's more excited than Mr. Petrie when he's lecturing us on photosynthesis," whispered Milton to Horace.

Horace did find Mr. Franken's behavior different from the other curators he had met at the museum. "I guess he's just excited to have visitors. It probably gets lonely in this place."

The kids finally agreed to the impromptu tour. But as they wandered through the first-floor exhibits, it started to feel like it would never end. Milton looked at his watch three times, but Mr. Franken didn't seem to get the hint.

"The museum holds over one thousand items, many of which I've personally collected myself. We have a large collection of artifacts from the archaeological dig over at Fort Saint Joseph. There is a case or two of pieces from the Potawatomi Tribe on the second floor. And you'll even find a dozen drawings by Chief Sitting Bull there. And on the third floor we have a room full of local memorabilia from some of our famous residents."

The phone at the front desk rang. "Oh, I'm sorry. I'm the only one here today," Mr. Franken explained. "I'll be right back."

Finally, a break, thought Horace.

Horace turned to his friends. "Quick, let's split up before he comes back. It might make it easier to find something. I'll take the third floor. You two, check out the second."

"Good idea, Horace. And less time stuck listening to this guy," added Milton.

Horace climbed the three flights of stairs, and then paused to think before walking into the gallery. He stopped at a display case featuring past town citizens. He was familiar with some of the names, like Ezekiel Niles, the newspaper owner, and Ring Lardner, the famous journalist. But toward the end of the display case was a whole section on two of the most famous industrialists in the town's history, Horace and John Dodge. Horace knew little about these brothers, one of whom shared his first name.

Looking at the Dodge display now, Horace noticed that next to a black-and-white photo of the brothers was the original insignia of their car company, with the words DODGE BROTHERS encircling the outside. On the top of the glass case was a placard that read FROM HUMBLE BEGINNINGS TO AUTOMOBILE BARONS.

Horace leaned in to read more about the two men. As it turned out, Horace and John Dodge had run a small metal shop in Niles before heading to Detroit. There they worked for Henry Ford, designing and building the chassis for his Model T. The two brothers eventually split from Ford and created their own company. They were hugely successful until their untimely deaths in 1920.

At the end of the display case was another black-and-white photo, this one of their shared tomb in Detroit. It was a giant mausoleum in the shape of an Egyptian temple. Surrounding the entrance were two sphinxes, and above the doorway was the winged disk of Ra.

"Interesting, isn't it?"

Horace jumped, startled by the voice.

"These two brothers were part of a rich past here in Niles. There is so much to learn about the town. So much history to be discovered." Mr. Franken's eyes were ablaze. "Do you have any questions?"

Horace hadn't even heard the curator approach. "Not

really. Just looking around."

Mr. Franken made a low snorting sound under his breath, seemingly frustrated by Horace's lack of interest. "Would you like to see what's in the carriage house? We have some wonderful old cars out there, one of them built by the Dodge brothers here in Niles. It never went into production, and I don't often get a chance to show it off. We're still working on the exhibit."

Horace was reluctant to leave the display case. He was fascinated by the photo of the tomb and wanted to learn more about it and the brothers and their mysterious grave. He was also a little jealous. There was a part of him that had always wanted a brother, someone to help level the playing field and be an ally in his battles against his sisters.

But it seemed Mr. Franken was not going to take no for an answer. "Come on, let's find your friends. I think you all will really like the car exhibit."

As they made their way back down the steps to the first floor, Horace saw Milton and Anna wandering around the second floor. He walked over to them. "Any luck?"

"Not yet. Where are you going?" Milton asked.

"The carriage house." Horace rolled his eyes over at Mr. Franken. "He insists. Come on."

Despite their protests that it wasn't going to help their search, the two joined Horace. Anna insisted that their best chance of finding more information about Keepers in Niles rested in the third-floor exhibit where he'd been earlier. Horace agreed and hoped their trip out to the carriage house wouldn't take long.

But when they reached the door of the carriage house, a bus pulled up in front of the main building, and a group of elderly patrons began to disembark. The sight of the new guests sent Mr. Franken into a tizzy. "Oh, no, you can't park there!" he called out, waving his arms wildly and running toward the bus. "I'll be right back, kids. You can look around inside. Just please don't touch anything until I return."

The kids nodded as Mr. Franken scurried across the parking lot.

"All right, let's just look around fast and then go back to the third floor. We don't want to get stuck on another one of his tours," said Milton.

The carriage house wasn't just an exhibition space; it also served as a storage unit for the overflow from the museum. Most of the artifacts were piled in boxes. "This is kind of a mess," Milton noted, stopping in front of a row of tarp-covered antique cars. "Must be someone's collection they donated to the museum."

Horace ducked under the first tarp. "It's a 1940s Ford truck."

Milton was already on to the next car. "This is a Chrysler Imperial. They don't make these anymore."

But when Anna got to a car at the end of the row, she suddenly popped her head back out from under the tarp. "You two have *got* to take a look at this! Grab the corners of the plastic."

Horace and Milton ran over, and with a swift yank, the three kids pulled the protective covering to the floor. Horace couldn't believe what he was seeing. It was one of the most bizarre-looking vehicles he'd ever laid eyes on.

"This is so cool!" Milton shouted. "It's called the Stout Scarab!" he read from a sign lying on the floor.

"Only nine cars were ever made!" Anna pointed to the

placard next to the car. "It was one of the last cars the Dodge brothers built together before they died."

The car looked like a steel missile, its lines curving in a smooth arc across the back aluminum fuselage. The kids began to walk around the car, marveling at its shape. The interior space was just as innovative as the exterior. The engine had been placed in the rear, freeing up the inside and creating a prototype for the minivan. Running boards lined the door panels, and wicker chairs were arranged around a table on the inside.

"This is amazing!" said Anna. "Do you still have your beetle?"

Horace pulled the beetle out of his pocket and held it up against the hood ornament. It was a perfect match.

"We've got to get inside!" exclaimed Milton.

Anna hesitated, but Milton had already sidestepped the flimsy red roping circling the car.

The door latches were embedded into the door panels, and it took him a minute to finally figure out how they worked. Milton flipped the latch and opened a door. "Come on."

Horace made his way around the roping, and Anna followed.

Milton started playing with a piece of plastic fruit and a tea set on the table near the back of the car. "Tea, anyone?" he joked in a British accent.

Anna didn't find it funny. "You guys, we are going to get in trouble. I don't think Mr. Franken will be too happy if he finds us playing inside one of his exhibits."

But neither boy was really listening. As Milton teased Anna about her manners, Horace made his way to the front of the car.

The speedometer was in the center of the console and surrounded by four smaller dials. A stick shift came out of the floorboards between the two front seats, and a key dangled from the ignition. There was a small glove compartment on both the right and left sides. Horace tried to see what was inside, but they were locked. But the most striking feature of all was the symbol on the center of the steering wheel—another scarab beetle.

"Guys, look," said Horace.

Milton and Anna stopped arguing and turned away

from the table. They moved to the front of the car.

"There's an indentation in the center of the steering wheel," said Horace, "like the one that used to be on the tree at the farm."

"Let's see if this thing still works." Milton reached forward and turned the key hard to the right.

"Milton!" Anna yelled in protest.

But nothing happened. The car didn't even make a beep.

"Relax, Anna. This thing probably hasn't worked in sixty years."

"More like ninety," said Horace, pointing to a date on the dashboard.

As his friends continued to bicker about whether the car actually still worked or not, Horace reached into his pocket and took out his scarab beetle. The stone beetle was glowing a bright blue light.

His friends stopped and stared in wonder.

Without saying a word, Horace instinctually knew what to do. The beetle was vibrating intensely in his hand. He placed it into the center of the steering wheel. Suddenly the car's engines roared to life.

At the sound of the engines Horace lost his balance.

"Be careful!" shouted Anna, but it was too late.

He fell between the front seats, knocking the stick shift. The car suddenly jumped forward. And in a giant flash of blue light, they were gone.

chapter six

When the brilliant burst of light had faded, the three friends found themselves stepping out of a lamppost and onto a dark city street corner. A soft rain created a fog across the pavement, and the sky was a deep shade of pink as the last rays of the sun disappeared behind the horizon. In the distance, Horace could see a pair of billowing smokestacks, and the strong smell of diesel was in the air.

"Look at that!" Milton shouted as a trolley car came rushing up the street alongside them. Passengers were hanging off the back, and a man tipped his hat as the car went by.

"Where are we?" asked Anna. "New York City?"

"I have no idea," answered Horace, "but I think we might have just discovered another portal."

"Hey, more importantly, where'd my sneakers go? Those shoes weren't cheap!" Milton said in shock, looking at his feet and the worn canvas shoes now on them. Horace noticed his outfit had also changed. He touched his head. He was now wearing a short-brimmed cap, the kind he'd seen newsboys wear in old black-and-white movies. A cotton button-down shirt was in place of his T-shirt, and a pair of three-quarters'-length wool pants had replaced his jeans.

"You guys shouldn't complain," Anna said. She was wearing an ankle-length skirt. "I can barely move in this thing."

Horace's eye caught the reflection from the street sign above their heads and the name Farnsworth.

"I don't know of any Farnsworth streets in Niles," noted Milton.

"Yeah, this isn't Niles," agreed Horace. "I'm pretty sure it doesn't have trolley cars." He looked down the street at the row of brick buildings. "If this portal works like the last one, Mr. Franken won't even know we are gone by the time he returns to the carriage house. Remember, time moves a lot faster on this side. Let's check it out. Maybe there is someone nearby who can tell us where we are."

The street was fairly nondescript. There was a trash can that stood on the corner next to the lamppost. A few discarded newspapers floated across the pavement, and a moldy half-eaten sandwich was smashed against the sidewalk. Two men dressed in tight-waisted jackets and skinny black trousers walked past the kids. Both wore dark hats pulled low over their eyes. When Milton started to ask them a question, neither paused nor said a word, only acknowledging the three kids with side-glances.

Horace was starting to wonder not just where they'd arrived, but when. Something about these men felt unsafe, and the idea of asking around suddenly seemed dangerous. The last thing he wanted to do was draw unwanted attention to them.

The kids walked up and down the block three times before they found a clue. Horace turned to see Anna cross the street to go stand at the door of a brick building.

The building was three stories tall, slightly larger than its surrounding neighbors. She waved for Milton and Horace to come closer.

The two boys ran across the street. "What is it?"

She was pointing up to the glass symbol set back in the center of the thick wooden door.

Horace's eyes opened wide. "It's the symbol of the Keepers."

"Down here, Horace," Milton added. The lock on the thick door was unmistakable. It was in the shape of a scarab beetle.

"I think someone's up there," said Anna, gazing at the second-floor window.

A shadow moved across a dim yellow light.

"We've got to get inside," Horace said in a determined voice. "This has to be connected to the beetle."

There was the distant sound of sirens, and now three men appeared under the lamppost. Anna and Milton were also feeling unnerved by their new surroundings.

"This place is sketchy," noted Milton. "Maybe we should speed things up."

Horace knew they needed to get off the street. Two of the men appeared to be the same guys who'd passed them earlier, and a third, much larger figure had joined them.

"If our clothes are any indication, I think we might be back in the 1920s. And that was the time of Prohibition and bootleggers," explained Anna.

"You mean mobsters?" asked Milton.

Anna nodded as the men started walking toward them.

Horace turned back toward the door and pulled out his beetle, blocking the glow of its light from view. He looked at the door lock and then again at the beetle in his hand. He paused for a second and then slipped the beetle into the lock. With a gentle twist of the knob, the door opened, and the three of them stared into the shadowy entryway of the building.

Horace could make out paint cans, a cotton canvas, and several ladders lining the dark entrance. They stepped over them as carefully as they could, tiptoeing inside. There on the left side of the hallway was a set of wooden stairs.

"Bring the beetle over here so I can read this in the dark," Anna whispered.

On a wooden table that looked to be a reception desk was a plaque that read THE SCARAB CLUB—FOUNDED IN 1907. There was a series of black-and-white portraits above the desk. Under the frames was a separate plaque of names of what appeared to be past presidents and the dates they served.

"Look," said Milton, pointing up. Above them, illuminated by the light of the beetle, written in white chalk and running along the beams supporting the ceiling were at least two dozen more names. "There's your name, Horace," noted Milton, indicating directly above them.

Horace could see his name written diagonally across one of the beams, and next to it was the name John.

"This is really strange, Horace. Did your grandfather ever mention anything about a Scarab Club?" Anna asked.

Horace shook his head.

"And we still don't know when or where we are," added Milton.

Horace wasn't certain, but he had an idea now. The names on the ceiling seemed to jar his memory. "You guys, some of these names look like the same people I saw at the museum in the third-floor exhibit." He was about to say more, when they heard a loud bang above their heads.

The kids looked at one another in alarm. "Maybe coming inside was a mistake," whispered Anna.

Bang! Bang! More sounds could be heard coming from the second floor.

"Let's get out of here," exclaimed Milton. But when they looked back at the open door, three shadowy figures could be seen on the street in front of the building.

Horace slammed the door closed and turned back to his friends. "First the Scarab car, then a portal, and now this, the Scarab Club. We are definitely on to something. We have to see what's up there." He grabbed the wooden banister. "Just give me a minute. You two can stay here. I'm only going to take a quick look and then I'll come right back."

"I've heard that before," responded Anna nervously. "I'm coming with you." She quickly lined up behind Horace as he began his ascent up the wooden stairs.

"I guess I'm coming too. I mean, what else am I going to do—try to make friends with those guys out on the street?" Milton added sarcastically.

Soon the three kids were quietly climbing up to the second floor.

Horace stopped on the landing. By the soft glow of the beetle, they could see trinkets and antique vases resting on a shelf along the wall. And mounted above those was an antique knife. It was roughly the size of an envelope opener, but its handle was etched with intricate designs.

Milton reached over and grabbed the knife off the two hooks holding it. "Just in case," he whispered.

Horace nodded, but Anna didn't seem pleased with the idea of Milton wielding a weapon. "You're more likely to hurt yourself with that thing than someone else. Be careful," she whispered back.

More banging noises rang out from the second floor, and the kids stopped halfway up the second set of steps. *Anything or anyone could be up there*, Horace thought. *Maybe we should have returned to the portal.*

But then it grew silent, and one by one they continued their ascent. It reminded Horace of the times when he'd tried to sneak into his sisters' bedroom. He'd learned from those excursions that the trick was to keep as little weight on his heels as possible. At least back in Niles the worst thing that awaited him was a disgruntled sibling; but here who knew what was upstairs?

They silently climbed another ten steps before reaching the second-floor landing. A large doorway was directly across from the landing. The door was open slightly, and Horace could feel a warm breeze slipping out into the hall. "Wait here," he whispered to Anna and Milton.

Horace walked across to the door and, closing his right eye, peered in through the opening with his left eye. He thought he could make out the outline of a table and the glow of a fireplace beyond it, the source of the warm air.

In a matter of moments, he decided it was worth the risk and slipped his fingers along the edge of the wooden doorframe to gently pull it open even more. He could now make out a mural on the opposite wall above the fireplace. A half dozen glass chandeliers hung from the ceiling, illuminating the room. Craning his neck, Horace could see names written on these ceiling beams too. He desperately wanted to get a better look at the names. If he wasn't mistaken, one of them looked to be his grandfather's name, Flinders Peabody.

He leaned in even closer, straining to get a better view. Suddenly the door burst open, and a hand reached out, yanking him into the room. Horace was about to let out a scream when he saw the face of the person holding him. He could not believe his eyes.

"Herman!"

CHAPTER SEVEN

"Horace!" Herman shouted in surprise, releasing his grip and embracing the boy in a giant bear hug. "You found me."

"Where have you been?" Horace responded, catching his breath and getting his bearings. "You've been gone, like—forever! I thought you were coming right back after you took Tut to Egypt."

"Sorry, I was sidetracked with other business connected to the Order. Tut's return didn't go as smoothly as I had hoped."

"Is he okay?" asked Milton. He and Anna had come into the room.

"Hello, you two! Nice to see you. Yes, back to Tut. For now he's safe. But there is a lot that still remains at stake," Herman answered.

"But what was all that banging earlier?" asked Anna. "It sounded like something was exploding up here."

Herman held up one of his shoes. "Oh, this." He slipped it back onto his foot. "Sorry, there was an annoying fly I was trying to kill."

The three kids laughed in relief.

"Enough of all that for now. Let me show you around." Herman raised his arm in a grand gesture. "Anna, Horace, Milton, welcome to the Scarab Club—the humble headquarters of the Time Keepers!"

The kids blinked in disbelief as they stared around the room.

Now Horace could clearly see a spectacular wood-paneled room illuminated by the fire in the stone fireplace. The room itself was impressive, but the most breathtaking feature was a beautiful mural painted above the fireplace. The central image was of a massive tree, much like the one at Horace's grandparents' farm. In the branches of the tree was a strange collection of objects painted in dramatic colors. From where Horace stood, he could see an hourglass, a book, a globe, a jar of brushes, and an old man's face. But before he could ask any questions, Milton started peppering Herman with his own.

"So, are you guys the same Time Keepers from Egypt?" asked Milton.

"Of course. I assume you already saw downstairs the pictures of our past presidents and the list of their names."

The three kids nodded.

"Good." Herman turned and with another sweeping gesture said, "And this is where we meet to discuss important matters of the day."

"This place is incredible," announced Anna.

"Make yourselves comfortable," Herman said, and he pulled four chairs to the table. A stack of giant poster-size sheets of paper lay across it. "Let me clear this out of your way." Herman began to flip through the pages, pushing them aside and making space for the kids. "The Order moved to the city over a century ago, but we only recently finished this building for our headquarters. A fitting place for the next few centuries," he said with a smile.

"City?" Horace pointed down at one of the pages. "Wait, are these maps of . . ."

"Yup," answered Herman. "Detroit. That's where you've arrived."

"Detroit! Awesome!" said Milton in excitement. "Maybe we can go to a Lions' game!"

"Milton, you've got to be kidding yourself if you think this is the twenty-first century," noted Anna. "I mean, look at our outfits."

"You're right," Herman said, resting his arms on the table and shifting comfortably in his chair at the head of the table. "The year is 1926. The Lions won't have their first season for another four years."

"1926!" exclaimed the three kids simultaneously.

"So we've traveled back to the Roaring Twenties?" asked Horace.

Herman nodded.

"I thought so," confirmed Anna. "The time of bootleggers and Prohibition!"

"That explains why those guys outside were so

sketchy!" exclaimed Milton.

Herman nodded. "Detroit is a booming city, but also one full of contradictions. The two biggest industries are the car companies and the bootleggers illegally smuggling alcohol into the States from Canada. I wouldn't recommend hanging out on these streets too long after the sun goes down."

"But why Detroit? Why the 1920s?" asked Horace. "And why are you here? Shouldn't you be back in Egypt?"

"There is a rich history to this place. What happens here in Detroit will change the world," explained Herman.

"Just like what happened in Amarna would forever change Egypt," added Anna.

"Exactly." Herman picked up a map from under the pile. Horace could see a grid of roads, and the city along the Detroit River. "But don't worry about all that now. I have a question for you three. How did you end up here?"

"Well," Horace said, then paused a moment before continuing. "I'm not totally sure. We went to the museum to see if we could find out more on Niles's history and the Keepers, and then we stumbled across this strange antique car called the Stout Scarab. It turned out to be some sort of portal."

"Yes!" exclaimed Herman. "The other end is the lamppost here on Farnsworth Street." Herman had a wide grin on his face. "Well done, Horace. It's not every day a Keeper is able to find a new portal without any help or clues."

"Actually, the reason we found the second portal in the first place is because something happened to the one out at the farm." Horace was reluctant to tell Herman that he had tried to go back to Egypt through the portal. Herman had warned him not to attempt it.

"What do you mean?" asked Herman, setting aside the map.

"Herman, I have to tell you . . ." Horace took a deep breath. "I was going to try to go through the portal to visit Tut. But when I got to the tree, I discovered that the portal had been destroyed."

A siren blaring in the distance seemed to correspond with the shock that now was spreading across Herman's face. "Wait. What did you say?" Herman gripped the table with both hands.

Horace was embarrassed to admit that he had been defying Herman's orders. "I'm sorry, I just wanted to check on Tut. I know it was a mistake," said Horace apologetically.

Herman was shaking his head. "No, no, no. Not about Egypt. What did you say after that?"

"The portal. The one at the farm, in the tree—it was destroyed."

Herman's shock now turned to suspicion. "You are sure you saw this?"

"Yes," Horace said defensively. "One hundred percent. I ran my hand over it. It looked like it had been carved out with a knife."

Herman shook his head. "This can't be happening." His eyes seemed to glaze over, and he was lost in thought.

"It's true," interjected Anna. "We went to the museum today looking for answers, and we found the Stout car. And well, that's how we found you."

Anna's words seemed to bring Herman back out of his thoughts. "I'm glad you discovered the car. The Stout Scarab was designed by two of our members to create a direct path between Niles and Detroit."

"Portals can be created by people?" asked Milton, confused.

"Not often. But the individuals who created the Stout car were especially gifted and"—Herman paused to emphasize the point—"motivated to find a direct path between the two towns, fulfilling a unique mission they'd been given by the Order."

But Horace was more concerned about the destroyed portal, and he redirected the questioning. "What about the portal at the farm, though? Do you know who could have destroyed it? Or why they would have done it?" added Horace.

"I don't know." Herman shook his head. "But it was no accident. The two things Keepers guard most are their portals and . . ." He reached into his pocket and pulled out a stone the color of an amethyst, placing it on the table. It was the size of a soft eraser and in the shape of a scarab beetle. The stone cast the whole table in a brilliant purple light.

Horace looked over at his friends, growing more

confused. "What? You have a scarab?"

"We all do," Herman said, and his eyes glowed from the reflection of the stone. "Each Keeper has his own unique beetle for opening the portals."

"So there *are* other Keepers!" Horace exclaimed at this revelation.

"Of course," Herman said with a nod. "The Order is very old, and these little beetles serve as our keys to this ancient network. Here, let me show you." He smoothed out the map he had pulled out earlier from the stack.

The kids gathered closer around the table. In the light of the purple beetle, other features on the map began to appear.

"Wait, are these . . . portals?" asked Anna.

Herman beamed. "Now you are figuring it out. When you opened the portal at the farm to go back to Egypt, you unknowingly joined a vast network of Time Keepers connected to hundreds of portals connected to thousands of places." Herman pointed down at the map. "It's hard to keep track of them all, but these portals jump from different cities to different times."

"Sounds like some complicated plumbing," said Milton.

"And there are places where multiple portals exist simultaneously. These are called vortexes. They are very powerful, energetic places. You could say they are the Grand Central of time travel," said Herman. "Detroit is one, and so is Niles."

"Is a portal like a time machine?" asked Horace.

"No. Time machines can move from any time to any place. The portals are fixed routes between a specific time and a specific place. For example, the tree leads to Ancient Egypt, but only Egypt." He looked back at the map and continued. "But when they are opened by a scarab, time within them begins to move again. It's like suddenly the ink in a history textbook can be erased or rewritten. Does that make sense?"

"Wow!" exclaimed Anna. "This is super complicated and sounds really dangerous."

"You're saying, when we move through a portal, we can change history?" asked Horace.

"Yes." Herman paused. "Time travel is not easy, and

it should never be done lightly. History is not written in stone. There is fluidness to the past that is far more susceptible to change and influence than many realize. In numerous ways the Order plays a role in guarding that flow and movement." Herman's jaw tightened. "In our heyday we could fill this room from wall to wall with Keepers. But things have become more challenging." Horace thought he saw some tears in his eyes, but then Herman quickly wiped them away. "Recent history has become more uncertain, and if what you say is true, Horace, things have become very dangerous. The Order isn't as big as it used to be, but the forces against history have grown strong. It's becoming more difficult to protect what we love." For a moment Herman seemed lost in his thoughts, then he continued. "To destroy a portal is the greatest act of evil one could take against the Order. We are all in great danger. I must get you back home. Immediately!"

Herman jumped to his feet, pushing his chair up against the wall.

"Wait a minute. You've got to give us more information," pleaded Horace. "You can't just stop there. If we hadn't found you, you would have never known about the tree portal being destroyed. And if the Order really is in danger, we need to know!"

Herman looked reluctant to say more, but Horace stood his ground.

"We aren't leaving until you tell us what's going on," said Anna, supporting her friend.

"Yeah," seconded Milton.

It became clear Herman was outnumbered and wasn't going to win. He pulled his chair back and sat down. Leaning over the table, he began speaking in a whisper, as if whatever evil forces were working against them stood just outside the door. "The worst thing anyone could do to the Order is destroy the portals." Herman looked straight at Horace. "It is not something I would like to imagine, but by doing so, it could potentially trap a Keeper on the other side of time."

"What's so bad about that?" asked Milton.

Herman took a deep breath and then released it. "I have only seen it once, and it is something I never want to see or think about again." He swallowed hard, gathering his courage. "But since you ask, I will tell you. Each of us has a life force we come into the world with. That life force is tied to a particular time and place. A Time Keeper is an exceptional human being because they have the ability to open the doorways between different times and places. However"—Herman now was pointing his index finger at one of the portals on the map—"one can never stay too long on the opposite side of a portal. The flow of time is strong, like a deadly current pulling beneath the surface. If you do, your life force will begin to weaken and"—he paused—"you will thin."

"You'll lose weight?" asked Horace.

"That doesn't sound so bad. My mom is always trying some new diet. I'm sure she'd be happy to get stuck in a portal for a little while," added Milton.

"No." Herman shook his head. "Not physical weight. You will thin like a piece of paper left out in the rain. Your strength will fade, then your thoughts . . ." He paused, emphasizing his next words. "And you will die." He stopped and sat back in his chair. "It was lucky you weren't on the other side of that portal when it was destroyed, Horace, but someone was hoping you were. A Keeper must always be careful how long they stay on the opposite side of time. The hourglass is merciless, and when the sand runs out . . . that's it."

Horace sat back, taking it all in. He had no idea about the specific risks of time travel. When he had traveled back to Egypt, he'd seen it as a great adventure. And yes, there were dangers in being in a far-off place, but actually having his life force drained out of him felt especially creepy. And he had put his friends in this kind of danger too! The thought sent a chill down his spine.

"Now you understand why I must get you home. If someone has destroyed the portal at the farm, they could just as easily destroy the portal you came through to find me."

The kids' eyes suddenly widened in understanding. Horace nodded. "Okay, we get it. But there has to be something we can do."

"Go back to Niles. Wait until my next message, and keep your eyes open for anything suspicious," said Herman. "That is enough for now. Hurry, we must get you back to the portal."

Anna and Milton said their good-byes to Herman and then started back down the stairs. Horace and Herman followed. Just before Horace reached the first landing, however, Herman reached out and grabbed him by the shoulder.

"Horace." Herman leaned in close so only the boy could hear his words. "Our enemies are dangerous. They stretch across history and will stop at nothing to destroy us. But there is something *you* can do for the Order." He looked around before continuing. "If the portals really are under attack as you say, I can't be traveling back and forth to Niles. It is too dangerous, even for me. I have to stay here in Detroit."

Horace nodded. "I understand. I'll be okay," he answered reassuringly. "I've got Anna and Milton, and Shadow. We'll watch out for any suspicious activity, just like you asked."

"I know you will." Herman paused to make sure the other kids weren't in earshot. "But I need you to do something else for me, Horace."

"Sure, what is it?" he asked.

Herman gripped Horace's shoulder firmly. "If the portals are destroyed one by one, our enemies will be able to isolate each of us. We will be helpless, and the Keepers will be wiped out forever." He leaned in. "But you know the true reason for the Order. It is more than just preserving individual pages of history; rather, we were created to safeguard the entire book."

Horace's eyes widened.

"We have guarded the Benben Stone across space and time for centuries, and we can't let it fall into the wrong hands."

"Do you think it's Smenk who's destroying the portals?" Horace asked, wondering if their old nemesis had returned from Egypt.

Herman shook his head. "No, I don't. He is dead. Very few people could survive the destructive power that Smenk unleashed in Egypt. I fear it is someone we didn't expect, someone on the inside, someone on the other end of the portal."

"You mean in Niles?" Horace asked.

Herman did not directly answer his question. "We mustn't make any assumptions. But I have a feeling the person who is destroying the portals is also seeking the Benben Stone."

"Why?"

"Because if they are systematically destroying the portals one by one in Niles, they might also know where the stone is."

"Wait, what do you mean?" Horace asked. "Didn't you take the Benben Stone back to Egypt, where Tut and the others could keep it safe?"

Anna and Milton were now waiting patiently down by the front door.

"The stone isn't in Egypt," Herman said. "It's in Niles."

Horace's mouth dropped open.

Herman leaned in. "And I need you to guard it."

Horace was overwhelmed with anxiety. For weeks he had been thinking about the Benben Stone and wondering why Herman wouldn't let him have it. And now Herman was saying that the stone had been in Niles all along? "But where is it, Herman? Back at the farm?" asked Horace.

"The museum?"

"No." Herman leaned closer. He spoke in such a low whisper that Horace could hardly hear him. "Go to the cemetery and find the Beeson Crypt. You'll know what to do when you get there."

chapter eight

The three kids emerged back in the carriage house just moments later. Luckily, Mr. Franken was occupied with the new tour group. They were able to slip out unnoticed, collect their bikes, and head back to their respective homes, promising to talk more at school the next day.

On his ride home, Horace was consumed by thoughts of what Herman had told him. The Order was under attack, and the Benben Stone was in Niles. Herman wanted Horace to protect it, but he warned him not to tell his friends. The more people who knew its location, he said, the more likely the stone and the people involved would be put in jeopardy. Horace wished he'd remembered to tell Herman about the dream, but with everything they had discussed, he'd totally forgotten.

Horace was also left thinking about the significance of the small town of Niles. Herman had said it was a vortex, a place where many portals converged. Horace had already discovered two, but he wondered what others might exist.

When he finally got home, Horace had a dazed look on his face, which he explained away by telling his mom he'd eaten a whole bag of gummy worms while at the movies with his friends. Horace kept a low profile at dinner that night, letting his sisters dominate most of the talking before he headed up to his room to reflect on all he'd learned.

Shadow was perched on his windowsill, and Horace threw an extra piece of turkey from dinner onto the ledge. As he thought about the task Herman had given him and wondered how he was to accomplish it, Horace was glad she was here. For a moment he stared out the window, lost in thought. The damaged portal at the farm was an unsettling turn of events. It meant that someone knew both about the portal and, even worse, the Keepers of Time. He wondered if they also knew about him. Herman didn't think so, and that's why he wanted Horace to stay away from the farm and not do anything that would draw curious eyes to him.

Horace could only think of four people in the whole town who knew of his role in the Order; two were his best friends, Anna and Milton, and the third was his grandmother. But there was one more person. The thought stuck in his mind like a piece of gum on a sidewalk after a hot summer's day.

Seth had stumbled upon the portal by chance. And even though he had proved a valuable ally to Horace and the others on their adventures in Ancient Egypt, Horace still wasn't sure he could be trusted. But as Horace thought more about it, he quickly dismissed the possibility that Seth was responsible for destroying the portal. Herman had made it clear that someone had deliberately destroyed the portal; this was not just a childish act of vandalism. And more importantly, since their return from Ancient Egypt, Seth had kept his distance, seemingly fearful of Shadow and of Horace and his newly discovered powers. His behavior at school earlier in the week seemed to prove that.

The last rays of the setting sun shone in through the window, but another light caught his eye. He looked down at the scarab now resting in the open top drawer of his desk. The beetle was nestled up against the old leather book from his grandfather's study. The scarab was glowing again, bathing all the contents of his drawer in a green light. *A green light again? Why?* thought Horace. It was strange, but his beetle only took on the green color in the presence of the . . . the book. The book! He hadn't given it much thought since he'd brought it home.

The book was small, not much larger than a journal or tablet. A small brass lock held the front and back covers closed. Horace had given the lock a couple of quick discreet tugs in the backseat of the car when they'd first driven home from the farm, but it refused to release. Now seeing the book resting in the desk drawer, with the glowing scarab next to it, he was determined to get it open.

He began to study the lock closely. Its brass metal was badly rusted, its opening almost invisible beneath a layer of corrosion and dirt. Slowly he traced out the edges onto his sketchpad. In doing so, he noticed that despite the rusted metal, the opening in the lock was almost identical to another object in his possession, the beetle.

Horace set the book down and ran into the bathroom to grab a cotton swab and some rubbing alcohol. He'd learned how to clean tiny gears from watching his grandfather over the years clean his collection of antique pocket watches. Using his fingernails, he began to scrape off the dirt in the lock. He dabbed the swab into a small cup of rubbing alcohol and slowly cleared away the corroded metal around the opening. He repeated this a half dozen times until an oval shape began to emerge from under the rust. It was a perfect match.

Horace didn't need to be told what to do next. It was just like the door to the Scarab Club in Detroit. He slipped the head of the beetle into the lock and turned it. With a loud clicking sound, the lock opened!

As gently as if he were handling a rare manuscript at the National Archives, Horace opened the front leather cover. The paper pages inside were coarse and thick. They had a faint floral smell. Strangely, there was no writing on the first page, not even a random ink splatter. He flipped through the pages faster and faster. There was nothing inside, just page after page of blank sheets. The only noteworthy feature was a half-torn page at the end of the book.

Horace turned back to the spine and saw the strange marking again. It was definitely the symbol of the Keepers, the eye of Horus.

Was this a journal his grandfather had owned but never used? Horace had a handful of journals in his own room, but all of them were filled, front to back, with sketches. It seemed odd that his grandfather would have had something so obviously related to the Order and not have used it.

He pulled out his phone and put the flashlight directly up against a sheet of the coarse paper. Maybe he could find a subtle marking or word to hint at the true purpose of the book. But as he examined it more closely, even under the intensity of his phone's light, he still couldn't see anything unusual. Horace then held the pages up to the window. He'd sometimes used this trick when he wanted to trace a picture. Still nothing.

Horace set the book on the desk just before the bedroom door suddenly opened.

"Have you ever heard of knocking?" he said sharply. He slammed the book shut and slipped it into the drawer.

But before he could close the drawer to hide the book, his sister Lilly was already prying. "What are you doing?"

She craned her neck to get a better look. "Is that one of Grandpa's books? I knew you found something when we were at the farm. You were acting so funny in the car."

"What do you want?" Horace asked, growing irritated and trying to deflect his sister's questions.

"Can I have your earbuds?" Lilly asked. "Archimedes has bitten through the wiring in mine, and they don't work." Archimedes was Lilly's cat. He often snarled at Horace whenever he came near Lilly's room. Hearing that the cat had actually eaten through his sister's headphones gave Horace a hint of satisfaction, considering the countless times the cat had turned one of his homework assignments into stuffing for the litter box. He sometimes wished Shadow would give the cat a good scare, but Archimedes was smart enough to stay out of sight whenever the falcon was around.

Horace reluctantly opened up another drawer and

grabbed a pair of earbuds. "Catch!" He threw them across the room, and Lilly snatched them out of the air. "Why don't you keep a better eye on your cat?"

"Just don't let Mom see you with that book. She's not going to be happy if she finds out you were taking things from the farm." Lilly raised her eyebrows in a knowing glare and then shut the door.

Horace turned back to his desk. He knew Lilly wasn't completely wrong. His mom wouldn't be happy if she found Horace with one of his grandfather's old books. But he wasn't planning on letting her find out, and he hoped Lilly wouldn't say anything either.

While his sister had seen the mysterious leather journal, he was relieved she hadn't noticed the glowing beetle lying among his colored pencils.

There was something very odd about this book. Odder than the rusted lock on its cover, or even the textless pages. He could feel the subtlest of vibrations on the tips of his fingers, the same feeling he used to get around the portal at his grandparents' farm.

Horace could hear footsteps again approaching outside

his door. He shut the book and locked it using the beetle. He slipped the book under a pile of scrap paper at the back of the drawer.

There was a knocking at the door.

"What do you want now?" he asked, growing more irritated by his sister's intrusions. "Did the earbuds not work?"

His dad walked in just as Horace shut the drawer. "What's that?"

"Oh, sorry, Dad," he said. "I thought you were Lilly."

"I'm afraid not," his father replied with a smile. "Your sisters are in their room, finishing their homework. But it's time for bed, champ. Tomorrow is a big day. Do you have your costume ready?"

Horace had been so distracted by everything that had been happening that he had completely forgotten. Tomorrow wasn't just any day; it was Halloween.

"It's in the closet," he answered.

"Good," his dad said, and smiled. "Wait until you see what I'm planning for the front lawn. I think the neighborhood kids will love it!"

Halloween was his father's favorite holiday. Every year his dad would spend weeks building pieces for an elaborate display. At their old house in Ohio, he had once turned the front yard into the bow of a pirate ship. Horace could only imagine what he had in store for this year, especially since they'd only moved to Niles a few months before. His dad loved to make big first impressions.

"Go brush your teeth and then get to bed." His dad gave him a squeeze on the shoulder.

Horace headed out to the bathroom, hoping to beat his sisters before they took over the sink with their elaborate nighttime rituals. Tonight, though, just as his dad had said, they were both still in their room when he started brushing his teeth.

After a few minutes Horace finished up in the bathroom. His dad had already turned off his light and was staring out the window. He moved to the doorway to leave. Horace quietly slipped under the sheets, hoping his dad wouldn't notice anything unusual about the faint green light peeking out from the desk's top drawer.

"Dad?" Horace asked.

"Yeah?" his father answered, pausing at the doorway.

"Can I ask you something?"

"Sure."

"Why do you love Halloween so much?"

His dad walked back to the edge of the bed. "That's a great question." From the hallway light Horace could see a gleam in his father's eyes. "You see, my dad wasn't around much when I was a kid. He spent most holidays working. Halloween was the one night of the year when he'd stay home, no matter how much work he had, and spend it with us." He bit down on his lip, and Horace suddenly realized where he'd gotten this habit. "I guess ever since then it has been a special night for me. It always reminds me of my father."

Horace had never known his dad's father. He'd died when Horace was very little.

"Do you ever miss him?"

"Every day."

"Do you miss home?" asked Horace.

His dad laughed. "You mean Ohio?" He shook his head. "No, Horace, this is our home now." He pulled the thick quilt at the edge of the bed over Horace's chest. "Get some rest. You've got a big day ahead of you." He bent down and kissed Horace on the forehead. "I love you."

It didn't take long before Horace was in a deep sleep.

Horace was back in the cemetery again, surrounded by the headstones. The two boys he'd seen last time were waving for him to follow.

He made his way along the now-familiar gravel path deeper into the graveyard. At the back was the mysterious tomb nestled into its place in the hill.

Horace followed the two boys up the marble step to the crypt's doors.

One of the boys smiled and motioned for Horace to pull the thick door handle. Horace lifted the iron ring and pulled.

The door opened, and with it a brilliant purple light spilled out from the tomb. Horace squinted against the blinding light and willed himself forward. As he stepped into the tomb, he felt the floor under his feet give way. He now was falling into a black abyss of space.

His plunge through the darkness seemed endless. He briefly saw the smiling faces of the two boys. And then he saw the face of his grandfather. The shape faded, and Horace continued to tumble. Next he saw Herman intensely studying a pile of maps. But the last face was the strangest of all. It was Mr. Franken, the curator from the museum. He was inside the Stout Scarab car. His expression held a look of frustration and anger. Finally, when Horace felt he couldn't fall any further, out of the darkness appeared an object he would have recognized from a thousand miles away.

Resting on a marble pedestal and casting a glowing purple light was the Benben Stone.

CHAPTER NINE

Horace awoke with the beetle on his chest. He had no idea how it had gotten there. He was certain he'd put it in the desk drawer before he'd fallen asleep. And the dream about the tomb and the Benben Stone further added to the unsettled feeling growing inside his head.

Horace tried to push the feeling aside as he walked over to his closet and slipped on his costume. His Halloween outfit this year was inspired by his adventures from the previous month. Using tinfoil wrappers, he'd created the intricate crown of an Egyptian pharaoh, complete with the image of the head of a cobra glued to the brow. For a neckpiece he'd made a cartouche with his name spelled in hieroglyphics, and he'd used a skirt from one of his sisters as a royal gown. As Horace stared in the mirror he thought his Egyptian friend would have been proud. He looked pretty good as King Tut.

He hurried downstairs to grab some breakfast, and then quickly headed over to school. The minute he walked into Mr. Petrie's classroom, Horace was greeted with a high five by his best friend.

"Horace, you look awesome!" Milton shouted. "Just like the real thing." He chuckled. "And trust me, I should know."

"You don't look so bad yourself," Horace said.

Milton was dressed as an explorer, wearing a wide-brimmed hat and a pair of reading spectacles he'd borrowed from his grandmother. He carried a small pickax he'd found in their garage.

"Are you allowed to bring that thing to school?" Horace asked.

"No one has said anything," Milton said. "But maybe I should keep it in my backpack."

Anna looked equally impressive, with a baseball jersey

and knickers.

"What team is that?" Milton asked.

"The Kalamazoo Lassies—they were part of the Women's League during World War Two. Don't you read your history textbook?"

"I try to avoid it if I can," Milton answered with a smirk.

The kids all laughed and found their seats.

Horace looked across the room and saw Seth sitting in his seat with a grin on his face. He and his gang of friends were all dressed like ninjas. Horace wondered what poor victim would be the target of their bullying and pranks later on.

But sitting in class, Horace struggled to focus on Mr. Petrie's lecture. And not even the thought of the costume party scheduled at the end of the day could distract him from wondering about the Benben Stone and his dream.

The morning was almost over when Mr. Petrie broke from his lecture. "All right, class, one last thing before lunch today. Time to head to the library."

Sixth grade in Niles, Michigan, was still considered part

of the elementary school, and most of their classes were with Mr. Petrie with one or two exceptions. Their weekly trips to the library were one of them. Horace didn't mind the trips to the library; in fact, he quite enjoyed them. Any escape from the monotony of Mr. Petrie's lessons was a welcome relief.

Horace joined Anna and Milton at the back of the line waiting to exit the classroom.

"You okay, Horace?" asked Milton.

"Yeah, yeah. Everything is fine. Why?" he responded, feigning indifference.

"What did Herman tell you up on those stairs?"

Horace shrugged. "I promised I wouldn't say." Horace bit down on his lip. "But if it gets serious or you guys are in danger, I'll tell you."

Milton didn't look satisfied by his answer, but the line started moving and cut their conversation short.

The school library was in the center of the building. Two long entrance ramps led down to it, one from the first-grade wing, and the other from the sixth-grade hallway. Opposite the ramps were five rows of bookshelves, each leading to the reading carpet. Next to that sat a cluster of six circular tables. The checkout counter was against the far wall, surrounded by a row of computers and Ms. Sophie's desk.

As Horace made his way into the library, Ms. Sophie's soft gaze put him at ease. "Can everyone please find a seat?" She gestured toward the half circle of chairs arranged against the back wall.

Since arriving in Niles, Horace had quickly discovered that Ms. Sophie was one of the nicest teachers at the school.

"Okay, let's get everyone to settle down. Halloween is such a fun time, full of mystery, and"—her eyes widened— "ghosts!" She paused, looking around. The class went silent, waiting for her to begin, and Horace's heart skipped a beat in anticipation. He loved a good ghost story.

She turned the cart next to her chair so the kids could see a collection of books on ghosts and ghost stories. She pulled a volume from the cart. "Michigan has a long history of ghost stories from the Whitney mansion in Detroit to the bloody battlefield of River Raisin. Here in Niles we have our own ghost story, and it dates back more than a hundred years. It's tied to the Beeson family.

"In 1870 Mr. and Mrs. Beeson had a son who died around his first birthday. Mrs. Beeson was so upset by the little boy's death that she had her husband build a beautiful crypt in Silverbrook Cemetery."

Horace's eyes widened. Was this the same grave Herman had mentioned?

Ms. Sophie continued. "The legend claims that Mrs. Beeson visited the crypt every night to feed and change the little boy. This strange ritual went on for months through the summer and into the fall. Then on Halloween night, while she was feeding the small corpse, suddenly an eye fell out of the baby's head. The woman let out a terrible scream and died of a heart attack that very night."

The entire class cringed.

"It is said that Mrs. Beeson and her baby are buried together in that tomb. And legend says that once a year, on Halloween night, the echoes of Mrs. Beeson's scream can still be heard in the graveyard. And if you listen carefully, you can also hear her little boy crying."

Horace felt a chill run down his spine. Was Herman

crazy? He wanted Horace to guard a haunted tomb!

"So remember to be on your best behavior tonight. You never know if Mrs. Beeson might be wandering looking for her son's eye."

The kids just sat there in stunned silence.

Ms. Sophie chuckled and put the book back on the cart. "Now, you still have a few minutes to look around and find a book before the period is over."

The story of the Beeson Crypt had filled Horace with a sense of dread. Had Herman gotten the graves confused?

He got up and was about to head over to the nonfiction section when Ms. Sophie stopped him. "I watched you listening very intently to that story." She paused. "You have a real interest in the history of Niles, don't you? Like your grandfather."

"You knew my grandpa?" Horace asked.

"Oh, yes. We were good friends. I was so sad to hear about his passing. Before I came to this school, I worked at the town library. I used to see him browsing the shelves. He must have checked out every book we had in the nonfiction section. He loved stories about Niles and Michigan, and, really, history in general." Ms. Sophie beamed. "It looks like you've been bitten by that same bug."

Horace wondered what else Ms. Sophie knew about his grandfather, but he was too shy to ask. As the weeks had passed since his grandfather's death, fewer and fewer people seemed to mention his name.

She patted Horace on the back. "Now, why don't you find yourself a good book? And remember, most ghost stories aren't true. We just tell them to give people a thrill."

"Thanks," Horace responded with a half smile. He really hoped for his sake she was right!

chapter ten

The rest of the afternoon went quickly. After lunch, Mr. Petrie followed up another lengthy lecture with a packet of reading handouts, and then at two p.m. they finally got to participate in the school-wide Halloween parade. Before Horace knew it, the clock reached three, and Mr. Petrie announced, "All right, class, happy Halloween."

The kids ran to their lockers, throwing the candy they'd gotten into their bags.

Milton turned to Horace. "Let's meet up around seven o'clock at my house. We can order pizza and watch scary movies. Sound good?" asked Milton as he tossed his backpack over his shoulder.

"Got it," said Horace.

When Horace got home, he could hear a heated conversation taking place in the kitchen. He walked in to find his two sisters arguing about their costumes.

"You can't wear those pants. Mom said I can wear them," insisted Lilly.

"But I already bought a shirt to go with them," answered Sara.

Apparently both girls wanted to wear some of their mother's old clothing to a Halloween party later.

"Mom, Sara is being a jerk."

"Not now," his mom said. "Can't you see I'm on the phone?"

Horace slipped past Sara and Lilly and sat down at the table to work on his homework. He was hoping to finish most of his science lab so he could enjoy the night and the rest of the weekend. While he worked, his mom seemed totally distracted by her conversation on the phone. She was talking and rummaging around the kitchen. Finally, after what seemed like an uncomfortable pause, she hung up the phone.

"What was all that about?" Lilly asked.

"Your uncle is trying to finalize the will and the estate papers. He needs to account for some of your grandpa's stuff and the books we donated to the library. He says that one of them is missing. Do you know anything about that?"

Horace shrugged as Lilly gave him a knowing stare.

"We brought everything down in boxes just like you asked," answered Sara as Horace pretended to be suddenly interested in the newspaper lying on the table.

Horace continued his work, and his mom started making preparations for an early dinner. After Horace finished his lab, he walked over to the counter and started helping her. He chopped an onion and then added it to the spaghetti sauce simmering on the stovetop. Ten minutes later his dad walked into the house, carrying several bags of supplies from the local hardware store. "Hey, guys," he announced, "you know what tonight is?"

"Halloween!" Horace and his sisters shouted.

"Now, to complete the final pieces of the display out front, I need your help, Horace."

Horace looked down at his watch. "Do I have to? I told my friends that I'd meet them after dinner."

"You've got plenty of time. It's not even six yet," his mom said as she put a handful of noodles into a pot of boiling water. "What's the matter? Why are you so antsy? Aren't you excited to help your dad with the decorations?"

"Yeah," Horace said unenthusiastically. "I guess I'm still thinking about Uncle George. I just don't like his selling all of Grandma and Grandpa's stuff."

"We already talked about this. While the will prevents him from selling the farm, he has every right to clean out some of the old junk."

"It's not junk, though," Horace said firmly.

His mom frowned. "I'm not going to fight with you. You've got to give it a break. A lot of that stuff needs to be cleaned out. You've been acting funny ever since we went back to the farm."

"Horace," Lilly said with a sneer, "why do you care so much about what's at the farm anyway?"

Horace gave his sister a side glare and returned to stirring the sauce on the stove top. A few minutes of silence passed as Lilly set the table, and then his mom served the spaghetti. Soon they were all eating and discussing the night ahead. Sara and Lilly were heading to Halloween parties with their friends, and Horace told his parents he was meeting up with Milton and Anna. Finally, after a long discussion about how much candy they were allowed to eat that night, Horace dragged a piece of garlic bread through the remaining sauce on his plate, devouring the last morsels of food. "Ready, Dad," he announced.

His dad had converted most of the front yard into an enormous cemetery with headstones and coffins. The climax of the scene was to be a mummy that popped out of a wooden coffin as kids stepped onto the porch. He needed Horace to help with the rigging, which would be triggered by a motion sensor planted next to the front door.

Horace followed his dad out to the front of the house. An eerie soundtrack was playing from an open window, and a smoke machine hidden under the porch pumped fog out over the yard. Horace could see Shadow perched on his window ledge above.

Before tackling the rigging, they first moved a pair of

coffins so that they perfectly framed the sidewalk leading to the porch. The rigging took a little longer than expected. The string running between the coffin and the front door kept getting snagged on the porch and rocking chairs as his dad tried to hide it from view. Horace had to admit that this was by far his dad's most elaborate holiday production and likely to cause some serious nightmares for younger children.

"All set," his dad announced, placing his hands on his hips and looking over the yard in pride. "Now, be sure to stop by with your friends before it gets too late. I want to make sure you get some good candy."

"Yeah, we will," Horace answered, jumping onto his bike. It was still light out, but he knew that the sun would set soon.

"Now, have fun!"

"Thanks." Horace looked down at this watch. He had just enough time to make one quick stop before meeting up with Anna and Milton. Ghosts or not, he was going to find the Beeson Crypt.

cHapteR eLeveN

Horace pedaled as fast as he could through the neighborhood, with Shadow diving in and out of the trees lining the street. The sidewalks were already teeming with kids in costumes. He rode down Sycamore Street out to the edge of town where Silverbrook Cemetery was located, spotting the outline of the cemetery gate. It was strangely similar to the gate he'd seen in his dream. He put the coincidence aside and looked down at his watch. He was going to be late meeting up with his friends. Pulling up to the gate, he stopped his bike and sent Milton and Anna a quick text.

In the fading light he could make out the silhouettes of several trees and a smattering of grave markers. Horace rested his bike against the cast-iron fencing. He heard a small rustling among the headstones as a squirrel ran past. He watched as Shadow dove down, nearly catching the little creature by its tail.

Then farther in the graveyard, he heard the rumble of an engine and saw a pair of headlights come to life. Horace ducked behind a bush near the gate, and Shadow swooped back up to take a perch on a nearby tree. A car was only a short distance away. The dirt road starting at the gate circled around the cemetery before returning back to the entrance. Horace watched as the car slowly made its way through the cemetery and then back out the entrance gate. As it left the cemetery, he could see that one of the tail-lights was broken.

Horace remained hidden for several more minutes until he was certain the car had disappeared down the street and no one else was in the cemetery. He was just about to reconsider his mission and return another time, preferably during the day, but a strong vibration coming from his pocket stopped him.

At first Horace thought it was his phone and that

Milton was returning his text. But as soon as he reached into his pocket, he felt the cool surface of the beetle. Horace pulled it out, and as he did a halo of blue light surrounded him. As he squeezed the scarab, the light grew even stronger, casting the entrance of the cemetery in a strange glow.

He could now see in front of him, running parallel to the main road leading into the cemetery, a small gravel walking path. It led into the wooded part of the cemetery. Horace knew that the beetle was being drawn toward something in the graveyard.

Shadow leaped from her perch and circled overhead. Her presence reassured Horace.

Holding the beetle out in front of him, he followed the gravel path into the cemetery. The rustling of the leaves on the trees and the rhythmic crunching sound of his steps on the gravel were calming. The trees in this part of the cemetery looked older. Their trunks had grown thick and wide, some even partially swallowing several of the tombstones. Horace imagined that they probably had rings in their trunks dating back hundreds of years to the settlement of the town.

One particularly old headstone caught his attention. It was teetering on the edge of a large root. He walked over to examine it. At first it appeared that nothing was on the stone. As Horace ran his hand against the coarse surface, he could hardly feel any indentations from the inscription's lettering.

He brought the beetle up to the stone like a flashlight. As the light of the beetle hit the surface, he spotted a small symbol on the stone. Horace blinked. He hadn't seen the mark earlier. It began to glow.

He turned to another gravestone only a few feet away and found the same glowing marker. *Could this really be happening?* Horace thought. He then ran over and peered at a third stone located farther down the path. It was only when he traced the marking with his fingers that he realized what he was staring at. There, in the actual center of the stone within the inscription, was the glowing eye of Horus.

Horace looked around and wondered if there were even more stones with the secret marking. He stretched out his arm, raising the beetle. As if on cue, another marker glowed behind a tree. And then another across the gravel road, and a third just a few feet behind him. He turned around and around. One by one, like fireflies awakening in the night, the sign of the Keepers began to glow on tombstones all around him. A sea of mystical light filled the cemetery.

Walking through the graveyard, Horace stopped now and then to peer more closely at some of the stones. He didn't know how or why, but the area looked familiar to him. He recognized some of the names from his school reports about Niles's history and local citizens. The first was Ring Lardner, the journalist who had exposed the 1919 World Series scandal. And next to him was Frederick Bonine, a famous eye doctor who had once seen over five hundred patients in a single day. Horace turned to the next-closest grave and paused. He crouched down. Unlike the other two tombstones, this one was more recent. And the ground was still relatively bare, the grass just recently beginning to grow. Horace froze when he ran his hands across the cold surface.

As he stared at the marker, he began to cry. FLINDERS J. PEABODY. It was his grandfather's grave.

He *had* been here before, and it wasn't the dream. He'd been out to this part of the cemetery for his grandfather's funeral. But that morning had been rainy, and Horace had been too upset. He had little memory of this place or the other stones surrounding his grandfather's resting place in the cemetery.

Even two months after his death, Horace desperately missed his grandfather. He kept the letter from him under his pillow and read it most nights before he went to bed. He so wished he could share these adventures with him. But he knew he'd never see his grandfather again or hear his voice. With his grandfather gone, his grandma in a nursing home, and the farmhouse completely empty, it felt like that chapter of his life was over.

He stood up and tried to regain his composure. Looking around, Horace suddenly realized how deep he had wandered into the cemetery and remembered why he was here.

An icy chill filled his veins. He would have broken out in a sprint, but the beetle in his hand started to vibrate furiously. It was dark now, and he needed to find the Beeson Crypt.

Despite every bone in his body telling him to leave, Horace continued forward, descending the small knoll where he was standing. There, buried partially in the side of the hill with a small brook that gurgled beside it, sat a mausoleum. Set a good twenty feet apart from any of the other graves, this tomb, Horace could sense, had something different about it.

As Horace approached the large tomb, the light from the beetle grew stronger, confirming his intuition. He could now see a pair of angel's wings above the entrance and the single word BEESON. This was the grave Herman had told him to find.

Horace slowed his pace and squeezed the beetle tightly in his hand.

There was a strong magnetic pull drawing him to the mausoleum. He was only a few feet from the wooden doors and could see a rusted handle. As he moved even closer he was certain that a small symbol glowed on the handle. It looked like the mark of the Keepers. Horace's heart began to race as he approached the tomb.

He walked up the step and onto the smooth marble

surface of the landing. As he neared, the Keeper symbol on the door handle became more prominent.

Horace held out his beetle, and it glowed an almost fluorescent blue light. He knew exactly what to do. He stepped forward and placed the beetle into the lock. Inside he could hear a clicking sound. Horace reached out with his hand and turned the handle, pulling at the door.

It slowly opened. A stale wind blew out of the tomb like a giant exhale. Horace pulled even harder, opening the door more. His jaw dropped open.

Of all the things that Horace might have expected to find in the tomb, none were as breathtaking and brilliant as the object that his eyes now beheld. There were no bodies and no ghosts. A single purple light illuminated the empty tomb. And resting in the center on a small altar was the source of that light, the mystical Benben Stone.

Almost immediately the stone began to pulse, inviting Horace to use his beetle and access its memories. He remembered its power from his last trip to Egypt. Horace was torn. He desperately wanted to learn more about the Order and its history. And maybe he could discover who the members who still existed today were. Herman had asked him to guard the Benben Stone, but he didn't say anything about Horace using it. But the answers to all of his questions could be found right there in the stone. It was like a living library!

Horace looked down at the small indentation in the surface of the stone's smooth granite. He slipped the beetle into the stone and immediately felt a deep pulse travel through his whole arm. The room was washed in blue and purple light.

The images began to pour out of the stone, one after another.

These images were from Egypt, more specifically Amarna. But it wasn't like the Amarna Horace remembered. Everything was different.

There were no armies, no people, no markets.

In one of the images Horace saw the pair of obelisks that he had used as a portal in the past; now both structures were reduced to rubble. The gate, the walls, the temples, the streets—everything was leveled. Even the granite lions that once lined the temple entrance were scattered in pieces across a desert landscape.

In the last image, farther out amid the city's ruins, Horace saw two figures with shovels in their hands, digging through the rubble. Behind them was a wooden cart filled with various objects. They stopped and reached into the sand. They pulled out what looked like a burlap bag. But before Horace could see anymore, the whole scene was washed out by a bright purple light.

CHAPTER TWELVE

After finding the Beeson Crypt and accessing the memories from the Benben Stone, Horace struggled to hide his discovery from his friends. It had been hard enough to lie about why he'd been so late to Milton's house on Halloween night.

Over the next several days Horace came up with a number of excuses to his friends about why he couldn't hang out with them. First he claimed he was busy helping his dad with work around the house. Then he told them he was having trouble receiving their messages on his phone. By the end of the week, Milton and Anna were clearly suspicious of his odd behavior, but they both left him alone.

During that week Horace used the time away from his friends to ride his bike back to the cemetery. Shadow was always nearby. The first time, Horace only circled the outside perimeter, wanting to see if anyone was inside. The second time, he entered and briefly rode past the Beeson Crypt. But by the weekend, the pull was too strong. He desperately wanted to open the Benben Stone again and access its memories. He wanted to know more about the strange images. Who were the two figures, and what was inside the bag they had pulled from the sand?

As Horace rode through the gate of Silverbrook Cemetery, past the tombstones at the front, and down the hill toward the creek in the back, his desire for answers was overwhelming. This time he parked his bike behind one of the bushes near the crypt, camouflaging it with fallen leaves. Except for Shadow circling overhead, the cemetery appeared empty.

Horace doubled-checked to make sure no one was near. Then he opened the lock on the crypt door using his beetle. Shadow descended from the sky and perched herself above the doorframe, watching for any unwanted visitors.

Horace wasted no time and walked directly to the stone. It glowed brighter as he approached, as if it were sensing the presence of the beetle. He was fairly confident at this point of what to do. He reached out and placed the beetle into the indentation on the top of the stone. As soon as the scarab made contact, images began pouring out of the stone.

The burlap bag appeared immediately. This time a figure was carrying it onto a felucca, an Ancient Egyptian boat. Horace recognized the boat from his history books, especially its lateen sail that was silhouetted by the moon. It was night, but behind the vessel the horizon was illuminated by a blazing fire. A city was burning along the shore. The men on the boat seemed anxious, scurrying from side to side as this ship set sail and made its way across the sea.

The scene faded into a mist of blue light.

When the next image appeared, Horace could make out a towering mountain in the distance. As the image came into clarity, a castle stood on the top. The castle was mounted firmly on the jagged cliffs. A path wound down from the high precipice to a field at the base, where a large army had gathered. From the dark brown color and size of the dirt patch on the otherwise green field, it appeared that the army had been camped there a long time. Soldiers were gathering wood and dragging huge limbs toward the center of the field.

The scene now faded into night, and the images were from inside the castle. There were three men arguing. Next to the men was a young boy. It was unclear what they were saying, but from the animated gestures and looks on two of the men's faces, they appeared to be trying to convince the third man of something. Another moment passed, and then the boy stepped forward. He pointed at a dark shape behind one of the men.

The man paused and then nodded. He reached behind him and handed the young boy the object hidden in the darkness. It was the burlap bag. The two other men bowed, and the entire scene disappeared.

In the next scene Horace saw two of the men and the boy again. It was twilight, and they were on horseback, and the burlap bag was being carried on one of the men's saddles. They were riding through a town. After several twists and turns through the dark cobblestone streets, they stopped their horses and dismounted in front of a towering building, a stone cathedral. This giant church was five times taller than any other structure around it. The young boy tied the horses to a post and waited in a square a short distance from the church.

The two men walked inside carrying the bag. The young boy stood there for several minutes. The light began to fade. He sat down against a small wooden trough, tucked his head against his chest, and closed his eyes.

Suddenly a light could be seen under the cracks of the cathedral door where the two men had entered. And just as quickly the light disappeared.

Then an even brighter light flashed from inside the cathedral, and soon it, too, was gone. Finally, after a lengthy pause, a third light blazed forth; this one was so bright that it illuminated a giant rose window high on the front facade. The glass became a dancing mosaic of blues, greens, yellows, and reds. The intensity of the light became so overwhelming that Horace was thrown back and knocked to the ground.

chapter thirteen

What Horace saw in the stone confused him deeply. And while Herman had warned him about telling his friends about the location of the Benben Stone, Horace decided that Herman hadn't said anything about talking to his grandmother.

The next day Horace decided to ride his bike over to the nursing home, hoping to get some answers. When he arrived at Sunset Living, a few cars were already parked along the curb. Horace locked his bike against the fence and walked inside. Not much had changed since his last visit a month before, when his grandmother had first revealed his connection to the Time Keepers and the true meaning of his middle initial.

"I was hoping to visit my grandmother," Horace explained at the front desk. There were a few decorations left over from Halloween scattered around the entrance, including a scarecrow slumped against the counter.

"Unfortunately, on Saturday morning visiting hours don't begin for another two hours. You'll have to come back later in the day, young man," the receptionist said, turning her attention to her computer.

Horace's face reddened. "Please, I just want to speak to her for a few minutes."

The woman looked over her shoulder at him, and from her expression, Horace could see she was weighing whether or not to let him in. "My boss won't be happy about this." She pursed her lips together, then after a long pause answered, "Okay, but only for a few minutes. All the residents have to get to physical therapy soon."

"Thank you," said Horace, exhaling with a huge sigh of relief.

"Who is your grandmother?" the receptionist asked.

"Amelia—Amelia Peabody."

"She just finished breakfast. I'll take you down to see her, but remember you have to leave in ten minutes."

"Sounds good," answered Horace. "Thank you."

"Okay, just let me get your signature."

He scribbled his name on the sign-in sheet.

"Now, right this way," she said, and she led him down the long hall to the residents' rooms.

The whole place had a familiar medicinal smell that burned the tiny hairs of his nostrils. Several of the rooms still had framed Halloween cards on their doors. When they reached the end of the hall, the woman turned into the last room, and Horace followed. On the door was a card Lilly had made.

Inside the room Horace's grandmother sat in a wheelchair, staring at her television set.

"Amelia, your grandson is here!" the woman shouted loudly over the blaring noise of the show on the screen.

Horace's grandmother made an indistinguishable grunt, barely acknowledging his presence. She turned her head toward the window.

"Some days are better than others," the receptionist

explained. "You are welcome to stay if you want, but I can also take you back to the lobby."

"It's okay. I'll stay with her a little bit." He knew that his grandmother's health was declining from what his mom had told the family. Dementia was a cruel disease that each day was robbing his grandmother of more and more of her memories.

The receptionist said, "Suit yourself. I'll come back in a few minutes to see how you're doing."

The woman walked out of the room, and Horace turned toward his grandmother. He sat down on the bed alongside her wheelchair. "Grandma, it's me, Horace."

Her response was totally unexpected. It was as if a light switch had been flipped.

She snapped to attention. "My goodness, what's taken you so long? I didn't think you were ever coming back. Come here and give me a hug."

Horace was caught off guard by the elderly woman's firm grip as she pulled him in close.

"Sorry I scared you," she said. "I just didn't want that nosy receptionist hanging around. It's the only way to get them to leave me alone."

Horace smiled.

"Now, come closer. Let me get a good look at you." His grandmother was barking out orders, just like old times. "Wow, you are starting to grow. I bet you are going to be a beanpole like your dad soon."

"Thanks. I hope so." Horace had always been small for his grade, and his grandmother usually knew how to cheer him up.

"It is so good to see you, Horace. So many kids have lost all their manners these days. I watch them come into this place and stare at their phones as they sit with their grandparents. A real shame." She tapped her finger on the edge of her wheelchair in a knowing manner. "So much they can learn from their grandparents, but no one has the time to listen." She adjusted the afghan around her legs and then turned back to Horace. "Now, what really brought you here? Does it have to do with the beetle?" she whispered.

"Exactly, Grandma." He jumped right in, knowing that he had limited time before the receptionist returned. "My friends and I found another portal here in Niles. This one was at the town museum. It led us back to Detroit."

"Ahhh, so you found the headquarters."

Horace's eyes widened. "Yes, we did!" he said in surprise. "You know about the Scarab Club and the Stout Scarab car?"

"Oh yes, your grandfather often used that portal to travel to their meetings. And Herman—he was always such a good friend to your grandfather and me. What is he up to these days? Is he still the head of the Order? Does he have his head in a book?"

"Actually, a map," Horace answered. "He is trying to figure out who is attacking the Order." Horace paused, then continued. "Someone took a knife and gashed out the keyhole to the portal at the farm."

"What!" She looked visibly upset. "This is serious." His grandmother stared intensely at Horace. "What about our possessions at the farm? Did you find Grandpa's old collection of books before they cleared out the house?"

"Yes!" said Horace excitedly. "I found one journal, but there was nothing inside."

She paused before speaking. "I'm not certain which one it is, but one of those books contains secrets connected to the Order. Your grandfather spent years trying to piece together the history of the Time Keepers and their connection to Michigan."

"Well, Uncle George donated the other books to the Niles Library," Horace said. "At least those he couldn't sell."

"You need to see if you can find the ones that were donated to the library. There is important information in them about the Order. You can't let them fall into the wrong hands." His grandmother motioned to him to sit closer. "Now, let me tell you what I know of the Order and its connection to Detroit. Like most major cities, a lot of history has been lost over the years." She paused and scratched her chin. "Or a better way to say it is that it is not lost, but *buried.* Over time, cities often built on top of their past. The role of the Time Keepers is to uncover that history and preserve it. And that's what happened in Detroit. You see, the location of the city was important to the natives who were indigenous to this land. They understood that there was power in the land."

"Like Niles," added Horace. "But why have the headquarters in Detroit?"

"Great question," she said with a smile. "When Antoine Cadillac first arrived, he brought with him the most valuable possessions of the Keepers. He and his knights built a secret treasury to hold them. But in 1805 there was a great fire. The fire wiped out a lot of the original city."

Horace's eyes opened wide.

"There are people who would give their lives, as well as yours, to find out the secrets of the Order and find that treasury. Keep an eye out for . . ."

Just then a nurse appeared in the doorway.

"Oh, please don't sit on the bed—we just made it this morning. And what are you doing here? It's not visiting hours yet."

Horace noticed his grandmother pursed her lips at the comment.

"I'm going to have to ask you to leave, young man."

Horace leaned over and hugged his grandmother.

"Bye, Grandma," Horace said.

And then his grandmother whispered in his ear, "Be careful!"

chapter fourteen

Horace was able to return home before anyone grew suspicious of his absence. He spent the rest of the morning helping his dad in the garage and wondering about the treasury his grandma had mentioned. What possibly could be inside?

For lunch he made himself a peanut butter and jelly sandwich and then ran upstairs to finish the last of his homework. When he was all done, he looked over at his phone and saw it was getting late. But he still had time before the library closed. He was desperate to learn more about Detroit and maybe find his grandfather's donated books.

He threw his completed homework into his backpack and then ran downstairs to the kitchen. "Mom, can I go over to the library?" he asked. "I won't be long. I just want to do some research for one of my school projects."

His mom looked up from her work. "Okay, but make sure you're back for an early dinner."

"Got it!" answered Horace, and then he ran out the door.

Shadow was waiting diligently in the tree in the front lawn.

Horace shouted up to the falcon, "Let's go! The library closes soon."

The Niles Library was located in the center of town, next to the museum. They shared a parking lot. As he arrived at the library's entrance, Horace looked over at the carriage house, wondering when Herman might return through the portal in the Stout Scarab car.

Shadow took a watchful position on the bike rack, and Horace walked into the library through the main entrance. At the front was the checkout desk and to the right were several computers.

"May I help you?" asked the librarian manning the desk.

"Yes, I'm looking for the donated books section."

The librarian frowned. "I'm sorry, but we don't let patrons rummage through donated books until they are at the fall fair."

"I'm just looking for some books that might have been donated to the library by mistake."

The woman seemed to hesitate, so Horace continued. "It was a collection from my grandfather's house. They were donated after his death, and one or two shouldn't have been given away."

Finally she conceded. "In the back by the bathrooms." She paused. "Do you know what you're looking for?"

Horace wasn't really sure. "I think it was nonfiction."

"If we have any new donations, they'd be over there in one of those boxes on the floor. We haven't had much time to sort through all our donations this fall, so they might be a little disorganized."

"That's okay. I can just look around," Horace answered.

He soon found himself rummaging through three big

cardboard boxes. From space exploration to cooking to self-help, there was every subject Horace could imagine. Apparently, people in Niles had a lot of extra books. However, there was nothing that looked like it might have come from his grandfather's house. In fact, most of the books looked brand-new.

Could someone have taken them already? wondered Horace.

He continued to scour the books, losing all track of time in his exploration of their contents. And then toward the bottom of the third box, he started to find what he was looking for: books on Michigan. He slowly began flipping through the book titles: *Michigan's Natural History, The Story of the Potawatomie.* And then Horace saw it, a beat-up book at the bottom of the box: *The Legends of Detroit.* This had to be one of his grandfather's books! It looked especially old and worn. The binding was starting to peel off. He opened the book and began to delicately flip through the pages.

The Legends covered numerous stories and myths connected to Detroit and its early colonial founding. But it also mentioned ghosts and the city's famous cemeteries. The mention of the cemeteries rang a bell in Horace's mind. If the Keepers were hiding the Benben Stone in a Niles cemetery, could they also be hiding a treasury in one in Detroit? His grandmother never told him, but he wondered what could be kept in the treasury. He could only imagine the riches, including gold and jewels, hidden in the vaults of the Time Keepers.

Just as he was starting to get excited, an announcement came over the loud speaker. "Please make your final decisions and head to the checkout desk. We will close in five minutes."

Horace looked in the box once again to see if there might be anything else of his grandfather's. But there was nothing. He bit his lower lip in frustration; his hopes had been so high. Had someone already taken any other books? Holding *The Legends* in both hands, he made his way to the front of the library.

"Did you find what you were looking for?" the librarian asked.

Horace hesitated. "Well, I think this is one of my

grandfather's books. Is it okay if I take it back?" He handed the book to her.

She looked at its worn cover. "Hmm, this looks interesting, but it's also in pretty bad shape. I think it will be all right if you keep it," she said, handing the book back with a smile.

"Thanks," said Horace. He put the book in his backpack and headed to the exit.

As he stepped out of the front door of the library, he saw someone exit the museum at the same time. It looked like Mr. Franken. He walked across to a car in the parking lot. The man's presence at the museum wasn't unusual, but something about Mr. Franken's car looked oddly familiar to Horace.

Mr. Franken jumped into his car and pulled out of the lot. As the car turned onto Main Street, Horace noticed the car had a broken taillight. *I've seen a car with a broken taillight before, just recently*, he thought. *But where?* And then it struck him like a lightning bolt—the cemetery! Mr. Franken had been the one driving around the cemetery! Horace had to follow him and see where he was going.

He jumped on his bike and began to pedal as fast as he could. Shadow was already up ahead, flying above the car as if she knew what he was thinking.

Horace made a diagonal line across the front lawn of the library. He then hopped the curb at the other end and landed back on the opposite sidewalk.

As he hit the concrete and popped out of his seat, he thrust down hard with his foot on the pedal. The light turned green, and Mr. Franken's car turned right. Horace powered after him. He couldn't let him escape.

This cat-and-mouse game continued for another ten minutes as Horace pulled closer to Mr. Franken whenever he stopped at a traffic light or a stop sign, only to lose him again when he accelerated down the street. If it wasn't for a particularly slow mail truck, Horace thought Mr. Franken surely would have gotten away. He was starting to feel tired, and his legs were beginning to burn from the effort. Mr. Franken appeared to be heading toward the outskirts of town. Horace was struggling to keep up under the extended effort. But just when Horace felt like Mr. Franken was finally pulling away, he made an unexpected turn into Silverbrook Cemetery.

It was only another minute or two before Horace also reached the gate of the cemetery. He could see the one taillight of Mr. Franken's car occasionally flash as the car slowly made its way through the cemetery. He decided it was best to take the next part on foot.

Horace hid his bike behind a bush near the gate and began to make his way deeper into the cemetery. Ducking from stone to stone so that he wouldn't be noticed, he slowly crept along to get a better look at the car.

Horace watched as Mr. Franken exited his car. The man was looking for something, Horace was certain of it. But what?

Shadow swooped through the tree branches overhead, and Horace moved closer to follow Mr. Franken. But as he drew nearer, Horace stepped on a fallen branch. The noise echoed across the cemetery.

Mr. Franken looked up as Horace ducked behind the nearest gravestone.

Horace waited another moment and then peered over the grave marker. Mr. Franken was pacing around the back of the cemetery again and then peering intently at the names on the neighboring graves.

Horace had to get closer, but there were no more hiding spots between him and Mr. Franken. Shadow landed on a grave marker near the man. He spotted her and became incredibly agitated, raising an arm as if to ward off an attack. Horace hadn't seen a reaction like that one since Shadow had teased Seth at the front of the school.

Horace thought the distraction might be enough to get him even closer, but Mr. Franken quickly returned to his car.

He turned the engine on and drove out of the cemetery. Horace waited a few minutes to make sure he was gone and then slipped out from behind his hiding spot. He ran down to the Beeson Crypt. He wanted to make sure it was still locked. He pulled on the door handle, and it remained firmly in place.

"What do you think Mr. Franken is up to?" Horace asked Shadow as she circled overhead in the late-afternoon sun. "I know it was him out here the other night. I recognize the broken headlight. Do you think he knows about the Benben Stone?"

Shadow let out a squawk.

"I know. I have to tell my friends, even if Herman warned me otherwise. It's too suspicious," Horace said. "Things are getting serious." He knew he couldn't keep doing this alone, and he needed to get help. He had to tell his friends no matter what Herman had told him. Mr. Franken was up to no good.

CHAPTER fifteen

It wasn't until lunch on Monday that Horace finally got his chance to apologize to Milton and Anna for his behavior over the past week. He walked to their usual spot in the cafeteria and sat down.

Milton slid over on the plastic bench, making extra room. "I didn't think you wanted to hang out with us anymore. I mean, you basically spent all last week avoiding us."

"I know," said Horace, blushing. "I'm sorry. I should have told you what was going on."

"It's okay, Horace," said Anna reassuringly. "If Herman told you to keep it a secret, you don't have to tell us."

Horace shook his head. "No, I think I really need to tell you guys what's going on. I don't think Herman realizes what's happening here in Niles, and I can't do this on my own anymore." Horace reached into his lunch bag and took out a juice box. He took a long drink from the straw and then cleared his throat.

Horace explained how Herman had told him about the Benben Stone and its hiding place in Niles and how he had found it Halloween night. He admitted he had been using his beetle to access the memories within the stone. He described the cryptic scenes he'd seen. He started with the ship sailing away from the burning city to the appearance of a mysterious burlap bag in the mountains. He told them about the cathedral filled with light and then, finally, how he'd followed Mr. Franken to the cemetery and seen him snooping around.

"I knew it was here!" exclaimed Milton. "But the Beeson Crypt! Isn't that the tomb that's supposed to be haunted?"

"Who cares about ghost stories, Milton?" Anna looked back at Horace. "I wonder what you were seeing in the stone. Last time you looked in it, the memories were

specifically about Smenk. But these seem bigger, connecte
to more than just a single person. I wonder if you wer
seeing memories of the stone itself."

"That's what I thought! The stone was revealing it
history to me."

"But why would the stone be sharing its history witl
Horace?" asked Milton, confused.

"Because maybe Horace is going to play a role ir
shaping that history," explained Anna.

"You are starting to sound like Mr. Petrie, always
harping on learning from the past so we don't make the
same mistakes in the future," said Milton.

"Mr. Petrie's not wrong," insisted Anna.

"You're right," agreed Horace. "My grandfather used
to always say the same thing. To understand who we are,
we must know where we came from."

"And to understand where we are going, we have to
know where we've been," Anna said with a smile. "My
mom says that, too."

The three kids paused, reflecting on what this might
mean.

Horace finally broke the silence. "Well, there won't be a future for the Benben Stone, at least not with us, if we don't figure out what Mr. Franken is up to."

"We need to go back through the portal at the museum and tell Herman."

"That's not a bad idea because the truth is, I wasn't totally honest with you either, Horace," Milton said, "and I feel pretty bad about it. There's something I have to return. I kept the knife."

"You still have it?" Horace said in surprise.

Milton nodded. "It's at home."

"Sounds like we're going back to Detroit, then," Anna said.

"Great!" said Horace.

"Let's meet there on Friday when the museum closes."

"Deal!" answered Milton.

CHAPTER SIXTEEN

Their break-in at the museum was planned for Friday night. They didn't want to draw any extra attention to themselves, and figured this was the one night of the week all three of them could get out of their houses with an easy excuse of going to the movies. Horace also promised Anna he wouldn't go back to the Benben Stone until after they had spoken with Herman. But on Thursday, Horace decided he wanted to check on his grandmother one more time.

After school Horace grabbed his bike and made his way over to Sunset Living.

When he arrived, he found his grandmother outside in

the rose garden with one of the caretakers. She was sitting in her wheelchair, the sun shining upon her face. She was wearing the softest of smiles.

"Would you like to help before she goes in for dinner?" the woman asked, noticing Horace as he rode up on his bike.

"Yes," Horace answered, hoping to have a few moments alone to speak with her. "I'll bring her down to the cafeteria."

"That would be really nice of you. I think she would like that."

The aide walked over to another patient, and Horace was left alone with his grandmother.

Horace reached down and pulled up the high-compression socks on his grandmother's ankles. They were meant to reduce blood clots and aid with her circulation. Both were a concern now that her mobility was dramatically reduced to spending most days in a wheelchair.

"Grandma, can I ask you something?" He was hoping to make sense of their last conversation, and he had a remaining question that had been lingering for days.

"Of course, Horace, what is it?"

"Back in Detroit, what was in the treasury? You never told me."

Without hesitating, she answered. "Why, the most treasured possession of the Keepers—besides the Benben Stone and the scarab beetles," she added with a smile.

Horace was frozen in anticipation.

"The lost prophecy," she continued. "A message from the original creators of the Benben Stone about its ultimate destiny. Anyone who was in possession of the prophecy would know the true purpose of the Keepers of Time and the ultimate destiny of the Benben Stone. That is why Antoine Cadillac and those knights brought the stone to the New World: to fulfill the prophecy." She paused, staring out over the lawn at the afternoon sun.

Horace's eyes widened in amazement. "That sounds incredible!" But as he processed the information, another thought came to mind. "Did Grandpa know about the treasury? Where the Keepers hid it?"

"That is what he was seeking this whole time." And then her smile faded. "But the Order has many enemies, and they have been looking for the treasury as well. Even in the Order, only a select group of members were tasked with keeping this great secret."

The mention of enemies raised another question in Horace's mind. "Do you know anything about Mr. Franken at the museum? Was he ever friends with Grandpa?"

She began to shake her head. "Not him, not him again." She started to grow agitated.

"What is it, Grandma?"

His grandmother now was looking off to the side. "I tried to warn you, Horace. Stay away from Franken. Stay away from him!" Her breathing became labored.

"Grandma! Grandma!"

Her eyes lost their brightness, growing cloudy, and it seemed she was no longer responsive. Horace called for help. "Help! Please help!"

Another aide sitting nearby with a resident came running over. "Can I assist you?"

"Yes, something's not right. I think my grandmother needs help."

The aide pulled out a phone and called for assistance.

Within moments another aide and a nurse appeared in the garden.

By now his grandmother was slumped over in the wheelchair, and her eyes had rolled back in her head.

"Grandma!" Horace shouted as he squeezed her cold hand.

As he moved closer toward her, the nurse intercepted him. "Please, I have to ask you to step back."

Suddenly Horace realized this wasn't just one of his grandmother's usual spells. Something was really wrong with her.

Horace stood at the back of the garden, frozen in fear. A nurse placed an oxygen mask on his grandmother's face. Then the elderly woman was moved to a gurney. A pair of paramedics crouched over her, pressing furiously against her chest. Minutes later they wheeled the gurney out of the garden. Horace watched as his grandmother was loaded into an ambulance. With sirens blaring, it soon rushed off.

Horace was in a daze. One of the nurses spotted him still standing in the garden and walked over to him. "I'm sorry, but I think you should probably head home now. We called your mother, and she is going to meet your grandma at the hospital."

"Was it something I did?"

"No." The woman patted his arm. "They will learn more at the hospital. There was nothing you could do. It looks like she had a stroke."

Horace didn't believe her. *I never should have asked her about Mr. Franken,* he thought.

CHAPTER SEVENTEEN

That night Horace could hardly sleep. His mom didn't come home from the hospital until after midnight, and he couldn't get the frightened expression on his grandmother's face out of his mind.

Friday morning Horace awoke to the sound of the kitchen phone ringing and the thumping of shoes on the wood floor of the dining room. It felt earlier than his usual time to go to school. Moving slowly, he put on his school clothes, then he brushed his teeth and matted his hair down with water. He was exhausted.

When he finally got downstairs, he found his mom talking on the phone, while his dad was quickly packing three brown lunch bags.

Horace sat down at the table and looked across at Lilly, who was eating the last of her breakfast. "What's going on?" he asked quietly.

"It's Grandma," Lilly whispered back. "They got a phone call earlier this morning. Things don't look good. They are moving her out of the hospital and putting her in hospice."

Horace crinkled his nose. "Hospice? What's that?"

Sara answered without even looking up from her phone. "Hospice is a place for the terminally ill."

"Wait." Horace paused. "Do you mean Grandma is dying?"

Sara nodded. "Her condition is worse, and the doctors think she now only has a few more weeks to live."

Horace's eyes widened. "What!"

"We just got the news, Horace. You've been upstairs this whole time," Lilly interjected.

Horace felt foolish for having stayed upstairs so long. He should have come down the minute he heard the phone ring. He knew it was odd for someone to call so early.

Horace ran his hands through his hair. What was he going to do? First his grandfather, and now his grandmother. If he lost her, he would lose not only one of his favorite people in the whole world but also the only family member who knew his connection to the Keepers. Even more than Herman, his grandma in many ways had helped Horace make sense of his role in the Order. She was the one who had told him about the treasury. She was the one who knew about the lost prophecy.

His mom rushed over to the table, interrupting their conversation. "Do the three of you have everything you need for school today?"

They all nodded.

"Good. Your dad and I have to go. We will be back later in the afternoon, but if you have any problems, you can reach us on our cell phones."

Horace was the first to break the silence. "Mom, what does all this mean? Is Grandma really dying?"

His mom sighed. "Unfortunately, the stroke she suffered is worse than they initially believed. We need to prepare for the inevitable. The doctors are now saying it is only a matter of time. . . ."

Horace swallowed hard and slumped down in his chair. How could this be happening again? He was just starting to come to terms with the loss of his grandfather, and he couldn't imagine a life without his grandmother, too.

"I'll call the school if anything changes. Okay?" his mom said. "But we have to go. The ambulette is coming this morning to move her."

Her comment only upset Horace even more. He remembered his first week of school. His mom had called the school office to make arrangements to pick him up early when his grandfather had died. Horace lowered his head, trying to hide the tears that were now running down his face.

He felt like this marked a shift in his own situation. First the appearance of Mr. Franken snooping around the cemetery, then his grandmother's warning about the man, and now her stroke. He was certain the events were connected and Mr. Franken was a danger to the Order. Maybe he had waited too long to reach out to Herman. Things were falling apart fast.

CHAPTER EIGHTEEN

The school day seemed to stretch on forever. Each time Horace looked at the clock to see what time it was, he felt like he was watching his chances to help the Order tick away with it. Herman had given Horace one task: protect the Benben Stone. But what about the treasury and the lost prophecy? Why hadn't Herman told him about these things as well? Horace was growing more and more antsy, finally finding the smallest bit of relief when the bell rang at the end of the day.

After finishing up his homework and eating some left-over pizza with his sisters, Horace met Milton and Anna outside the Four Flags Inn, an abandoned hotel on Main

Street. The hotel was located just opposite the museum's parking lot, and the kids thought it would be best to meet there first before heading to the museum.

"Horace, are you sure you really feel up to this? I know it has been a hard day," said Anna sympathetically. Horace had told them earlier about what had happened to his grandmother.

"Yeah, Anna is right. We don't have to do this tonight. We could come back another time," added Milton.

"No," said Horace firmly. "I've waited too long as it is. We've got to warn Herman about Mr. Franken."

"Okay," answered Milton, turning back toward the museum across the street. "Mr. Franken usually leaves by six p.m.," he said. "I've been scouting the place out for the past week."

Sure enough, just on cue the last light went off in the upstairs office, and they could see Mr. Franken as he made his way out the museum's door and got into his car. The parking lot was empty.

"Okay, let's go," Horace said.

The kids snuck around the building, keeping close to

the shrubbery.

"Let's try the carriage house's entrance," Anna suggested. "That way we can go straight to the portal."

Soon the kids found themselves at the door to the carriage house.

"How do you guys think we should try to open the door?" Horace asked.

Milton pulled a clothes hanger from his coat. "I brought this in case we needed to jimmy the lock."

Horace walked up to the door and jiggled the handle. It popped open immediately. "Hey, it's unlocked!"

Milton looked confused. "Weird."

"Is someone still here?" Anna asked. "Are you sure that was Mr. Franken we saw leave? Maybe it was another worker?"

"No," Horace said with certainty in his voice. "It was Mr. Franken. I'd recognize that car anywhere." The broken taillight had become an unmistakable marker.

"I don't know," answered Milton. "But all the lights are off. Maybe they just forgot to lock it up."

The kids cautiously walked into the dark building.

The red glow of the exit signs illuminated the interior just enough so they could make their way around without crashing into any of the exhibits.

"And there's no alarm," noted Horace. "This is a lot easier than I thought it was going to be."

Milton pulled out his phone and turned on a small light to illuminate the path ahead.

"Hey, look at this. This door is marked 'Basement.' I wonder if there are more things in the basement," said Anna.

"Great. We'll check it out later. But first we need to find the portal," insisted Horace.

The kids made their way to the back of the large room, where the cars were stored under their tarps. They walked past the line of vehicles until they came to the Stout. Its plastic cover lay on the ground just where they'd left it from their last trip through the portal. "Come on," Horace said.

He was just about to open the car door, when off to the side something caught his eye. It was an open box piled high with books. "Wait! What are these doing here?" He ran over, quickly flipping through the covers. They were some of his grandfather's old books! Mr. Franken must have taken them from the library before Horace had gone there.

Horace started to turn back to Milton and Anna, but before he could say anything, something hit the back of his head. Everything went black.

chapter nineteen

"Horace. Horace," the voice repeated. "Wake up." A cold splash of water came across his face like an icy bath in Lake Michigan.

Horace struggled to open his eyes. A throbbing pain filled his head as a blurry face swam in front of his eyes. "Dad?" For a moment he wondered if he was at home in bed; but then he realized he was on his side with the cold ground underneath him. He thought he heard the sound of leaves rustling.

The voice laughed, and another cold wave of water hit Horace in the face.

He tried to move his arms but realized they were tied

behind his back. He struggled to sit up.

"I caught you sneaking around the museum." Horace's vision cleared, and Mr. Franken's face came into view. "You think I'm so stupid to leave the Stout Scarab unwatched. The only reason I haven't destroyed that portal is because I'm waiting for Herman to show his face back here again."

Horace's head still ached, but he began to look around desperately. He knew he was no longer in the museum, but where had Mr. Franken taken him? From the rustling sounds and the tall shadows around him, he thought he was out in the woods.

"Where are my friends?" Horace demanded, twisting and turning to look for Anna and Milton.

Mr. Franken bent down. "They are back at the museum. I knocked them out as well and tied them up in the carriage house. I'll deal with them later." His face darkened. "But now I need you."

Horace looked around and suddenly realized where Mr. Franken had brought him. It wasn't the woods; it was Silverbrook Cemetery. Parked across from where he lay was Mr. Franken's car. Horace felt the cold marble against his back and now realized where he was—Mr. Franken had tied him up against the front of the Beeson Crypt!

Mr. Franken walked over and poked Horace. "You are now going to help me."

"Get your hands off me!" Horace yelled. "I'm not helping you." His shirt was soaked from the cold water, and he was starting to shiver.

Mr. Franken smiled. "But you already have. I circled back on foot after you saw me leave the cemetery, and I followed you to this tomb. I never would have discovered where Herman had hidden the Benben Stone if you hadn't shown me. And now you will do one more thing for me."

"I'm not going to help you get into the tomb," responded Horace, guessing Mr. Franken's next move.

"You think I need help getting into this building? Fool, the Order was great at *hiding* their treasures, but they never knew how to protect them." He walked to the trunk of the car, opened it, and pulled out a thick crowbar.

"Herman did his best to keep that information from me." He laughed a hollow-sounding cackle. "But I had no idea there was another one of you. And the fact that

Herman left *you* to guard the stone? I can't believe it. As a Keeper, I also know you have possession of a beetle."

"I don't know where it is," answered Horace. He knew he was a terrible liar, but he hoped it might be enough to fool Mr. Franken. "I don't have it."

"Don't lie to me," responded Mr. Franken. He walked over and began searching Horace's pockets. With his hands tied behind him, Horace couldn't stop the man. It didn't take long before he discovered the beetle, and he soon pulled it out.

"It will never work for you!" shouted Horace. "It's mine." Only a Keeper would be able to use the sacred scarab beetle. He'd learned that by watching Smenk struggle to use his beetle back in Egypt.

Mr. Franken smiled. "I bet Herman forgot to tell you something very important. You see, I'm a Keeper as well. Well, maybe, *was* is a better word. Let's just say my interest in finding treasure was stronger than my interest in protecting the Order or its mission. Unlike our other members, I saw the potential for power and wealth in the Benben Stone. They were only concerned with knowledge and history."

He went up to the door of the tomb and, using the crowbar, began to strike at it. It only took a few hard blows before the old handle with its lock shattered. Mr. Franken threw the crowbar aside and pulled the door open, stepping inside the tomb.

Instantly he was bathed in the familiar purple light emanating from the Benben Stone. Horace craned his neck to see inside. Mr. Franken turned back to look at the boy and smiled a knowing grin.

Horace watched in stunned silence as Mr. Franken reached out and inserted the beetle into the stone. He kept his hand there, holding the beetle in place.

But before Horace could think through the significance of this act, he found himself frozen by the images emerging from the stone.

Mr. Franken turned toward him. "You know there is a treasury the Keepers have kept secret for centuries, and within it is a great prophecy. Your grandfather knew about it. And with your help, I'm going to access the power of this stone and discover the treasury's location. And along with it, the prophecy. With that information,

I can destroy the Order."

Horace tried to pay attention to what Mr. Franken was saying, but his mind was occupied on another question. How was Mr. Franken able to use his beetle, Horace's beetle? Didn't the beetle belong just to him? Hadn't Herman said that each Keeper had his or her own beetle?

Mr. Franken was quickly moving through the memories like a master artist. "Show me the treasury," he whispered into the stone.

An image of a cemetery appeared—a different cemetery than the one they were now in; yet there was something familiar about the place. It was one Horace was sure he'd seen before, but he couldn't remember where. Then suddenly, as he peered deeply into the memory, Horace realized why the graveyard was familiar. And from the expression of recognition on his face, Mr. Franken apparently knew it as well. It was the same cemetery that was featured in the photo in the museum. Why was the stone showing them this strange place?

Horace knew he needed to stop Mr. Franken from further accessing the stone's memories and discovering the treasury and its ancient prophecy. But how?

He then heard something rustling just a few feet behind him. It was Shadow. Somehow she had found him. She must have followed Mr. Franken's car over from the museum. She was slowly walking toward him.

"Shadow," Horace whispered, "come help." He turned his back to show his bound wrists. "Here, Shadow."

The falcon didn't need any further direction. She hopped across the marble to Horace. Then she lowered her beak and began pecking at the thick rope. Horace didn't think he'd ever get free at this pace; the bird's movements were too slow and deliberate. But then, as if sensing his anxiety, Shadow redoubled her efforts and began to tear at the knots with both her beak and her claws. The rope started to shred, and Horace was able to wiggle his hands to loosen the bindings even more.

As soon as his hands were free, Horace felt a wave of relief. But he kept his hands hidden behind his back so that Mr. Franken didn't realize what had happened.

It didn't matter, though; Mr. Franken was totally consumed by the images now projecting from the stone.

His attention seemed to be captivated by one image in particular, a strange Egyptian-style tomb in the cemetery.

Keeping his gaze on Mr. Franken, Horace slowly began to slide himself toward the open door of the crypt. Even with the man's back to him, he still felt vulnerable. But Horace decided he had to take the risk. He had to stop Mr. Franken from going farther into the stone.

Reaching the doorway, Horace could see that Mr. Franken and the Benben Stone were still at least a dozen feet away. He jumped up and sprinted as fast as he could across the slick marble floor, hoping to take the man by surprise.

But the crackle of a leaf under his foot gave away his approach. Mr. Franken suddenly turned, raising his left forearm with a force that Horace hadn't expected. The full brunt of the blow sent Horace smashing against the hard stone of the crypt's wall. He slumped against it. Horace tried to catch his breath, pondering his next move, when Shadow suddenly swooped in behind him and started beating her wings in Mr. Franken's face.

The distraction from Shadow gave Horace a second

opportunity. He jumped back to his feet and, with the full force of his body, slammed his hand against Mr. Franken's hand holding the beetle in the stone.

"Get your hands off it!" Mr. Franken screamed. "Let go!"

The two were now battling fiercely to gain possession of the small beetle. It fell from Mr. Franken's grasp, sliding across the floor. Shadow swooped in agitated circles just above their heads.

Horace scrambled after the beetle and grabbed it with his right hand, but Mr. Franken was behind him, pulling at his ankle. Mr. Franken's grip was far stronger than Horace had expected for someone his grandfather's age. Horace twisted and turned, trying to get back to his feet. But he was yanked back to the ground by Mr. Franken.

Mr. Franken was now dragging Horace closer to him, while the boy did everything he could to keep the beetle out of reach. But the man was too strong. He grabbed Horace's hand and pried the scarab beetle out of his fingers.

"Got it!" he shouted in victory. He leaped to his feet and then gave Horace a hard kick to the stomach. The force of his kick caused Horace to curl over, coughing. Shadow landed next to his side.

Mr. Franken turned back toward the Benben Stone while Horace struggled to catch his breath. "If I didn't need you so close, I would have let you rot away with your friends in the carriage house. But this beetle won't work without you nearby." He paused and turned his attention back to the stone resting on its altar. "Once I find the secret location of the treasury, I'll also find the lost prophecy, and your usefulness will be over."

Mr. Franken didn't waste any more time, and he quickly reopened the Benben Stone.

But Horace wouldn't be so easily defeated. He used the last of his strength to straighten himself up. Shadow flew up from her place on the floor, hitting Mr. Franken in the head with the full force of her wings. As the man was thrown off balance, Horace saw his opening. He grabbed the beetle from Mr. Franken's hand. But just as Horace gained possession of it, Mr. Franken pulled at his shirt. Trying to steady himself, Horace reached out with his other hand and grabbed the closest thing to him, the Benben Stone.

Suddenly the Benben Stone erupted in an intensity of light that Horace had never seen before. The light filled the entire room, and in the next moment Horace felt himself falling forward.

chapter twenty

Horace hit the ground hard and heard Mr. Franken land with an *oof* behind him. He looked around. They were no longer in the Beeson tomb. They were in a grassy area, lying near a circle of stone obelisks. However, the obelisks weren't Egyptian, like the enormous ones Horace had seen in Amarna. These were smaller, each only six or seven feet tall and resting on a granite base. Horace realized one of them must be another portal. Behind the obelisks were headstones. Turning around, Horace could now see that they were in a cemetery. And behind the headstones was a huge mausoleum in the shape of an Egyptian tomb, with four papyrus-topped pillars framing the doorway and a pair of sphinxes flanking the stairs.

But which cemetery? Where are we? Horace wondered. Had they fallen into the memory?

Horace spotted Mr. Franken lying only a few feet away. And there in the grass between the two of them was Horace's beetle.

Mr. Franken was the first to react, and he immediately grabbed the beetle. He turned to face Horace with a look of triumph. "No more birds to help you, young Keeper." He brushed the dirt off his pants. "You opened the portal in the Benben Stone, a rare ability." He smiled a sinister grin. "You didn't know the stone itself was a portal—it's probably the most powerful portal of all. I'm surprised you were able to muster such magic, but even fools get lucky. And you have taken me right where I wanted to go."

Horace's face revealed his confusion.

"Don't you recognize this cemetery?" Mr. Franken continued. "We have its picture in our museum. I've been searching for the treasury for many years, wondering if this might be the location. I do believe we are back in Detroit, and if I'm correct, we have arrived in the 1920s."

So we are in Woodlawn Cemetery? But how? Horace thought. He remembered it from the museum photo.

"The Keepers like to keep their treasures with the dead. Fitting place, because soon you are about to become one of them." Mr. Franken smiled again. "They hid the Benben Stone in Niles, but the treasury was always here in Detroit. I should have known it was in Woodlawn. And you can only find the treasury when you go back in time to when it was first hidden." Mr. Franken began laughing. "The stone holds all the secrets. It always has. I just didn't realize you were going to make it so easy for me."

"I'm not going to help you."

"You sound just like your grandfather," Mr. Franken said. "When he kicked me out of the Order, he created an enemy he could never have imagined. I waited patiently for my opportunity, and I finally got it."

He looked around, holding the beetle in his hand. "And I can't think of a better place to get my revenge." He walked over to the obelisks. "You see, each one of these obelisks acts as a portal. This is a massive vortex. Let me show you."

Mr. Franken walked over to one of the stones and placed Horace's beetle on a marking halfway up its face. Suddenly a burst of light flashed from the stone, like a light bulb exploding, and a portal opened.

"See?" Mr. Franken said with a sneer. "I don't just destroy portals; I also open them."

Horace looked at Mr. Franken in shock. "It was you! You were the one who destroyed the portal in the tree at my grandfather's farm!"

"Of course it was me." Mr. Franken stepped back from the open portal and advanced toward Horace. "I'm sure you learned from Herman what happens when a Keeper gets stuck in the past." He smiled and pulled a piece of rope out from his pocket. "Fortunately, I have a little rope left over from tying you and your friends up."

Mr. Franken swung the rope over his shoulder. "Don't make this hard. It will only be more painful for you."

He charged toward Horace.

Horace dove behind one of the headstones, hunkering down out of view. He could hear Mr. Franken's heavy breathing on the other side of the headstone. There had to be a better place to hide.

But then a hand snaked out, grabbing his ankle. "Gotcha!" Mr. Franken shouted.

Horace kicked as hard as he could, sending the heel of his shoe right into Mr. Franken's nose.

"You little brat!" Blood spurted from the man's nose. Horace ran behind a larger monument, but Mr. Franken anticipated the move and came around the other side, blocking his way.

"Fine, I don't need to wait and let time take the life force from you. I'll kill you myself." He wiped his nose with his sleeve. Horace tried to duck again, but Mr. Franken was too fast. He grabbed Horace by the neck and began choking him.

Horace thrashed briefly, but he could feel the air being blocked from his lungs. His head pounded, and his sight seemed to dim. Things around him—the cemetery, Franken—were fading away. In one brief spark, his whole life flashed in front of him. All the memories, the adventures: he saw his family, his friends, and his grandparents.

Then abruptly Horace felt Mr. Franken's grip relax.

Air entered his lungs, and his breath deepened again. He shook his head to clear his eyes. He blinked several times to confirm what he was seeing. A ghostly shape seemed to be standing next to Mr. Franken's shoulder. And then a second one appeared on the man's other side. Now they were pulling Mr. Franken backward, away from Horace. Mr. Franken started to scream. As Horace watched, the two shapes dragged the man across the grass to the second portal he had opened.

"Please don't! Please don't do it!" The ghostly figures pried the beetle from his hand and tossed it into the grass. "I'll die there!"

The two figures did not respond. With a single movement, they threw Mr. Franken through the open portal. A brilliant burst of light flashed, and then the obelisk returned to stone.

Horace looked around. He couldn't believe what he had just witnessed. Mr. Franken had just been sent to another world, caught in a trap of his own making.

He walked over and picked up his beetle. He looked over at the mausoleum where the two ghostly shapes now stood. Horace recognized it from the picture at the museum. Above the door was a single word, DODGE. To his surprise, the door slowly swung open. The two shapes motioned for him to follow them into the tomb.

Horace walked behind them, ascending the steps. As he entered the tomb, he saw two marble sarcophagi, one on each side of the room. On one was written the name JOHN and on the second the name was HORACE. Slowly, as if by some ancient magic, each stone coffin slid to the side of the mausoleum, revealing a set of stairs that descended below.

"You must choose which path you would like to follow," a voice said. Horace swung around. The two ghostly figures were now standing behind him. Horace's heart started to race.

"One path leads to knowledge, the other to riches. Choose wisely."

Horace could see a golden light coming from one set of steps, while the other glowed green.

This must be a test, he thought. *I must decide whether I want the riches of the Order or its knowledge.* Horace began to pace around the tomb.

He had to choose. If he selected the riches, it could help his family and save the farm, but if he chose the second set of stairs, it might be the path to the prophecy.

He looked at the beetle and thought of all he'd experienced. He remembered the scarab had glowed green back at his grandparents' farm and whenever it was near the journal. Maybe his grandfather had been trying to tell him something all along. He thought about all the lessons his grandfather had taught him through the years. And he thought about what it meant to have real wealth in this world. It wasn't about possessing gold; it was about wisdom.

Horace walked over to the set of stairs that glowed green. As he descended beneath the tomb, it felt like the stairs seemed to go on forever. The walls became narrower and narrower, closing in on him. Just when Horace had thought he'd chosen the wrong path, he found himself entering the most surprising of places. He was in his grandfather's study.

But this room didn't look the way it had at the time of his grandfather's death. It appeared to be the study from a much earlier time. There were some books on the desk, and the grandfather clock ticked loudly in the corner, but there were also three portraits hanging on the wall and at least a dozen pieces of papyrus rolled up in the corner. There was also a gyroscope on one of the bookshelves and an antique marble bust sitting on the desk. Neither of which Horace had ever seen before.

Even the leather journal he had found weeks ago was there on a bookshelf, along with all the other books that had belonged to his grandfather. But they were all new. A lit lamp was on the wooden desk, and sitting beneath it was a torn piece of paper.

"You have chosen wisely, young Keeper."

Horace turned around to see the two ghostly figures reappear. "Who are you? You were in my dreams. You showed me where the Benben Stone was."

"I'm Horace, and this is my brother, John. We've been watching you for a long time."

"The Dodge brothers! But how? And where am I?"

"You are in the treasury hidden here in Detroit. We went to a great deal of effort and expense to build and guard this space, hiding its magic beneath our tomb."

"But this is my grandfather's study," explained Horace. "I thought there would be riches here."

John, the second brother, spoke. "Few have ever entered this space, but for those who do, it will always take the form of what feels most comfortable. When I used to enter it, it would often look like my old workshop from Niles. For others, it might resemble a monastery or a temple. For you, it is a mirror image of a place that is closest to your heart, your grandfather's study. And the riches are what you make of it."

Horace pulled the leather-bound journal from the bookcase. "I have this at home, but it's blank."

"Not as blank as you think," responded Horace Dodge. The ghost walked over and pointed at the torn page on the desk. "Here, I think you need this." He handed him the piece of paper. "A missing piece to an old puzzle."

Horace looked at it in confusion.

"When you return home, use the beetle to illuminate what others can't see. Then you will understand the magic and power available to you within this book," said John.

"But I have so many questions. Where is the prophecy? What happened to Mr. Franken?"

"Your friends are anxiously waiting for you to return. And I promise we will meet again soon," said Horace Dodge.

John pointed to the beetle in Horace's hand. "The beetle can take you to the past and bring you back to the present. But, Horace, your gift and destiny will be found in the future."

Now Horace Dodge spoke. "Look into the Benben Stone when you return. There is an answer to your question about the lost prophecy." He pointed to the piece of paper Horace held. "A prophecy you have had this whole time."

chapter twenty-one

Horace emerged from the portal in the Beeson Crypt and found Milton and Anna standing nearby in the cemetery. Their wide-eyed expressions showed their astonishment. Next to them stood Herman, Shadow perched on his shoulder. Immediately the falcon let out a loud shriek and circled over Horace. The three friends ran over to greet him.

"Thank goodness you're safe!" exclaimed Horace.

"Horace, you look like you've seen a ghost!" Milton noted.

"I think I did—actually two."

"You're okay. That's what's most important." Anna

gave him a big hug. "I think Mr. Franken knocked us out before he got you. When we woke up, we found ourselves tied up on the floor of the carriage house. We saw that you were gone. But then Herman appeared through the Stout Scarab portal and freed us."

"Yeah, and luckily I remembered what you said about the cemetery and the Benben Stone, so we came out here on our bikes," said Milton.

"Herman rode yours," said Anna with a smile. "It was a little small for him."

"So Mr. Franken must have knocked me out at the museum and then driven me out here in his car," Horace explained. "That all fits. But how did you know to come and help us?" Horace asked, turning toward Herman.

Herman nodded. "As I studied the maps of the Keepers, I noticed more and more of the Michigan portals were being destroyed. I realized it was only a matter of time before the portal in the Stout Scarab would also be destroyed and my chances of coming back permanently blocked. I couldn't take that risk."

"But Mr. Franken was waiting for you to come through

the portal in the museum. That's why he never destroyed it," said Horace.

"He must have thought he could use Horace to get what he wanted and then catch you later," said Anna.

"But where is Mr. Franken?" asked Milton.

"It was strange." Horace paused for a moment, trying to piece everything together. "When I woke up here, Mr. Franken stole my beetle. He used it to open the Benben Stone. I got loose, and we fought over the beetle, and then . . . I don't know how it's possible, but I think we fell, or traveled, through the Benben Stone—I guess it's a portal or something."

"Yes, it is very possible, but few Keepers can accomplish such a feat," Herman said.

"But how is that even possible?" asked Horace. "I thought it just held memories."

"Your passion for history and the past is so strong, so real, that the stone must have sensed it." Herman narrowed his eyes. "Tell me one thing, Horace, and it must be the truth. Did you open the Benben Stone on your own since we last spoke?"

Horace bit down on his lip. "Yes, I did. I just wanted to get some answers."

Herman nodded but didn't seem to be upset. "I probably would have done the same if I'd been in your shoes. I can only imagine how difficult it must be to feel all alone here in Niles and with questions no one can answer completely." His eyes softened. "The stone is like a living book, and it wanted to show you the answers to your questions." He paused. "What were you thinking about when you touched the stone?"

Horace furrowed his brow. "I think I was worried that Mr. Franken might find the treasury of the Keepers."

"Where did you end up when you traveled through the Benben Stone?"

"Back in old Detroit. In Woodlawn Cemetery. It turned out to be the location of the treasury." Horace hesitated. "But the treasury wasn't full of gold or jewels or anything like that. It contains whatever the person visiting it is hoping to find," answered Horace.

"Then what did Mr. Franken want with it?" asked Milton.

"He wanted to find the lost prophecy," Horace answered.

"But how did Mr. Franken know about any of this?" asked Anna. "How did he know about the treasury, or the Benben Stone, or a lost prophecy?"

"And how was he able to open the Benben Stone using my scarab beetle? Not even Smenk was able to do that back in Egypt," Horace said.

"He was once a Keeper," Herman explained. "And he must have used Horace's life force to trick his beetle into letting him open the Benben Stone. If he could get Horace close enough to the stone, his life force would be strong enough to power the beetle."

All three kids look stunned by Herman's revelation, especially Horace, who now understood what he had been feeling as he watched Mr. Franken open the stone. He had literally been drawing strength from Horace and using it to access the stone and its memories. The thought made Horace dizzy, and he swayed a bit. Anna rushed over to his side.

"Horace, you should probably sit down," she said.

Horace nodded and sat on the cool marble step at the front of the tomb.

Herman looked over at Horace. "Now, it is important you tell me everything that has happened since I last saw you."

Horace told him all that had happened that night. How when he came to, from being knocked out at the carriage house, he'd found himself in the cemetery lying against the Beeson Crypt. He went on to explain how Franken had broken into the crypt and, using Horace's beetle, opened the Benben Stone searching for the treasury. He described their fight for control of the beetle and how he had somehow activated the Benben Stone portal. He told of them ending up in Woodlawn Cemetery in front of the Dodge mausoleum. There Franken had revealed that he was the person who had destroyed the portal at the farm. Horace struggled as he told them about Franken's attempt to kill him. He finally ended by describing how the ghosts of the Dodge brothers appeared, saving Horace and trapping Franken in another portal.

"Where did they send him?" Anna asked.

"No one will know for certain," Herman said, and then he added, "unless he appears in the pages of history."

Milton and Anna cringed.

"But why did the Dodge brothers come to rescue me in the cemetery?" asked Horace. "I thought they were dead."

"As a Keeper, we are sworn to protect, to guard, and to care for the past. But we are also tasked with the responsibility of taking care of one another. Like a family that stretches across time, we must always be willing to come to the aid of another Keeper if they are in danger or call for help," Herman answered. "The Dodge brothers must have known you were in grave danger. And even as ghosts, they came back to the world of the living to help you."

"But what did Mr. Franken do to upset the Order?" asked Horace, remembering what his grandmother had said in their last conversation.

Herman pointed inside the tomb to where the Benben Stone sat on its altar. A deep purple light pulsed from within the stone's core. "You are strong-willed like your grandfather, and while you risked great danger accessing the stone without permission, I think you are ready. You deserve answers. And the stone is anxious to share them with you."

Horace looked at the Benben Stone and then down at the beetle in his hand. It glowed a bright blue.

"The answer to that question resides as a memory in the stone." Herman paused. "It may be painful, but the truth of the past is never something that should be avoided."

The other kids looked at Horace. "Go ahead," Anna whispered.

Horace bit down on his lip and stepped up into the tomb, toward the Benben Stone. He was afraid. He had seen its powers. And he feared what the stone would reveal.

As if reading his thoughts, Herman said, "Look deeply. It wants to share the story." The stone was starting to pulse more rapidly as if mirroring Horace's own heartbeat.

Horace nodded and placed his beetle into the stone's indentation, locking it into place. Suddenly the stone erupted in light, and Horace was momentarily blinded. But soon, within the depths of the light, he could begin to see images form. These images were familiar. It was like flipping through the pages of a living book. He saw the Scarab Club in Detroit; he saw the building of the tomb in Woodlawn; and the burial of the Dodge brothers. Finally, he found the memory he was seeking. He dove deeper into it.

Horace saw his grandfather. He was standing with Mr. Franken inside the carriage house of the museum. Both men appeared to be in their twenties. Horace watched then as his grandfather pointed to the Stout car, got into it, and disappeared into the portal. Mr. Franken moved to follow him, but before he, too, disappeared, Horace could see a scarab beetle in the man's hand. It was black.

The next scene flashed, and now both men looked older. They were in the wood-paneled room at the Scarab Club, standing across from each other at the table. They were arguing, and Horace's grandfather was visibly upset. Horace could hear his words. "You cannot be so careless. The portals are not your personal gateways to the past for collecting trinkets and treasures. If you leave them open again, we will all be in danger."

"I've been searching for the treasury as part of my mission to guard our Keeper history. Just tell me the location, and I won't have to go searching around."

"That is not for you to know. The treasury possesses all the secrets connected to the Order. You have yet to prove yourself as a worthy Keeper of that information."

Mr. Franken slammed his hands down on the table in visible frustration. "I'm not a child. Stop treating me like one."

"I will when you stop acting like one," responded Horace's grandfather.

Then a third scene appeared, showing Horace's grandfather and Mr. Franken. They were in the Scarab Club, standing in front of the fireplace. Shadow was perched on his grandfather's shoulder. Mr. Franken looked humbled. His eyes shifted nervously from side to side.

"I warned you," stated Horace's grandfather. "You can't go wandering through the portals out of your own personal interest. You have continued to defy our rules and guidelines. We are protectors of history, not collectors. Relinquish the beetle."

"But I won't do it anymore," Mr. Franken pleaded.

"You have said that before, but I will not give you such leeway again."

"No, no!" Suddenly Mr. Franken's eyes flashed with anger. "You are foolish; you have never realized the power we have. The way we could change history if we wanted to! No, I will never give you my beetle!"

As if responding to an unspoken command, Shadow swooped across, slashing Mr. Franken down his left cheek. The wound began to bleed. As the man put a hand to his face, Horace's grandfather wrenched the beetle from Mr. Franken's other hand.

"It is over." And with those words, his grandfather took the beetle and threw it into the fire. There must have been some great magic there, because the beetle exploded in a shower of sparks, unlike anything Horace had ever seen.

And then the memory dissolved into darkness.

Horace staggered backward, struggling to grasp what he'd just seen. He turned toward Herman. "I don't get it. If Mr. Franken was expelled from the Order, why did you allow him to stay here at the museum?"

Herman let out a deep sigh. "Your grandfather was a good and fair man; he wasn't cruel. He thought he could keep an eye on Mr. Franken if he stayed in Niles. And none of us thought he would be a threat without his beetle." Herman paused. "But we were wrong. His desire for revenge was far greater than we imagined. I'm sorry. Mr. Franken was able to use your beetle. He drew upon your life force to wield the power of the scarab." Then Herman looked sad. "You may have been harmed because of it."

Horace said, "It's okay. I'm a little tired and maybe a little sore, but nothing a little Halloween candy can't fix."

They all laughed.

"Seriously, though." Horace paused and then continued. "One last question, Herman."

"Yes, Horace."

"Are there any other Keepers in Niles?"

Herman nodded. "One."

"Who?" Horace asked, almost jumping out of his shoes in excitement.

"It is not for me to say." Herman turned to the other two kids. "It is getting late, and I think it is time you all head home. Your parents must be worrying." He paused. "And, Anna and Milton, because you now know where the Benben Stone is kept, you, too, are responsible for its security. You have proven to be great friends to Horace and to the Order."

Milton gingerly raised his hand. "Actually, I might not have been a good friend." He reached into his pocket and pulled out the knife he had taken from the Scarab Club. He handed it to Herman. "I may have borrowed this."

Herman smiled. "Thanks. I wondered where that had gone. I'll be sure to return it. Take care of one another. Horace is lucky to have such loyal friends. And the Order will need your help soon. The time is coming when we fulfill our ultimate mission. A destiny that has awaited the Keepers since their original creation. And the three of you are going to play an important role. Now it's time for you to go home and for me to return to Detroit."

"How are you going to get back to the museum?" Horace asked.

"I'll walk."

"Are you sure?" said Horace. "You can use my bike."

"I've spent some time in this town. I know my way around." Herman smiled, then took a deep breath. "And this will give me a chance to think about all I've learned tonight from you and your friends."

Herman followed them to the gate of the cemetery, and the three kids each gave the man a hug before saying a final good-bye.

Horace and his friends rode their bikes back into town. But before they went their separate ways, they stopped at the edge of Horace's neighborhood. He turned to Anna and Milton. "Thanks for sticking by me even when I was acting like a jerk."

"Anytime!" answered Anna.

"We've always got your back," added Milton. "Just don't keep any more secrets from us."

"Don't worry," Horace answered. "I won't."

Shadow circled overhead.

CHAPTER TWENTY-TWO

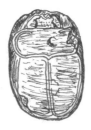

When he returned home, Horace had to answer a few questions from his parents. His mom was growing weary of his constant excuses of being at the movies, and now coming home later than expected did not help things. As a result, she promised a long weekend of chores. He took his punishment quietly and headed upstairs to his room.

Shadow was perched back on the window ledge. Horace closed his door and walked over to his desk. He opened the top drawer and saw the leather-bound journal. He had completely forgotten to tell Herman about the book! Now he pulled it out and looked at it closely. There had to be something special to the book; he could feel it in his fingertips. The Dodge brothers told him to look at the book in the light of the beetle, but what did that mean?

He pulled his beetle from his pocket and set it next to the book. The beetle began to glow green. Maybe his grandfather had encrypted the text so only a Keeper could see. But how would that work?

As before, Horace slipped the end of the beetle into the lock, and with a loud click, it opened. The front cover flipped to the side, surprising Horace and causing him to jump back. It was as if a wind had blown through the window, knocking the book open.

Horace placed the glowing beetle back down and stared at the open book before him. Something was different this time. Where before there had been a blank opening page, now he thought he could see the faint outline of letters. They were forming one after the other as if being written by an invisible hand. He rubbed his eyes to make sure he wasn't seeing things, then he picked up the book and stared at it closely. The page now seemed blank. He lowered the book, placing it once again next to the glowing beetle. The page suddenly came to life. The letters were only visible in the light of the beetle!

He could now see not just letters, but complete words and sentences. They were written in his grandfather's hand.

Horace began to read.

The Order traces back many centuries and spans from one end of the globe to the other. The members have come from many walks of life, many different families, and have been blessed with many unique talents. These men and women sacrificed their lives to fulfill an ancient prophecy.

Horace leaned over the text with growing excitement. It was all here, the whole history of the Order.

He returned to the book and began skimming through the pages and randomly stopping.

As the centuries passed and the Eighteenth Dynasty came to a close, the pharaohs of Egypt lost their rule over the land and people. The Keepers made the decision to move the Benben Stone out of the old temples and to the vaults at the library of Alexandria.

However, with the Roman occupation in the late third century and the rise of several power-hungry emperors, the safety of the Benben Stone could no longer be guaranteed.

In secret, while the city of Alexandria burned, the Benben Stone was moved across the Mediterranean to the mountains of Southern France. It wasn't until many years later, in the thirteenth century, that the Benben Stone resurfaced once again. One great cathedral, Chartres, was meant to serve as a new home for this treasure. However, when the French king discovered the stone was in his midst, he desperately sought it.

In the 1700s, under the guise of an exploratory mission, a group of Knights Templar, accompanied by Antoine Cadillac, brought the Benben Stone to the New World. After many months exploring the shores of the Great Lakes, the knights found a home for the stone in a small eastern settlement called Fort Pontchartrain. This fort eventually became the great city of Detroit.

Horace couldn't believe what he was reading. It was a larger explanation of all the images he'd seen in the Benben Stone. His grandfather had written everything down. Had he seen the images too? He looked over at the beetle, which was still glowing strong, then turned back to the pages.

Detroit grew into a hub of cultural prosperity and technological innovation. Members of the Order financially supported many of the city's great buildings, including the art museum, the main branch of the public library, the opera house, and the Scarab Club. However, the booming success of the auto industry in the 1920s, which helped fuel a renaissance of the city, also put the secrets of the Order at risk. What had once been a quiet outpost on a newly formed country's frontier had transformed into the economic and industrial epicenter of a burgeoning superpower. Detroit was now drawing the attention and interest of the whole world.

While the Headquarters of the Order remained at the Scarab Club in Detroit, the tiny town of Niles soon became a second home for many of its more important members. However, the Order made the decision to hide its greatest secret in a treasury within Detroit's oldest cemetery. That secret was a lost prophecy that dated back millennia.

Horace flipped to the final page of the book. He had almost forgotten what the Dodge brothers had given him back in the treasury. He reached into his pocket and pulled out the torn page.

He placed the piece of paper into the book. It perfectly aligned with the rest of the page. *It's the missing piece to an old puzzle*, Horace thought. He was about to grab some tape, when the beetle began to glow even brighter. Horace picked up the beetle, setting it on the page where the two halves met. A single beam of light shot out and began to weave along the torn edges. Like a needle sewing a seam, the light from the beetle fused the two pieces together right before his eyes.

Looking closely, Horace couldn't even see where the two pieces had once been separated. Now he began to read the text that had been missing for so long.

The ancient gateway to the stars is located along the banks of a great river that flows as the border of two lands. When the gateway is opened, it will offer a path to return the stone back from where it once came.

Horace sat back stunned. He couldn't believe he'd actually put together the pieces of the prophecy. Despite the hundreds of thoughts that ran through his mind, he was suddenly overwhelmed and exhausted.

He closed the leather journal, locked it with the scarab beetle, and slipped it back into the drawer. He'd solved enough riddles for one day.

After turning off the light, Horace slipped into the comfort of his sheets. The minute his head hit the soft down of his pillow he immediately fell asleep. But in his sleep a hauntingly familiar dream greeted him.

Horace was back in the graveyard of Silverbrook. But unlike his previous visits, the gravestones were all gone. In their places stood people, dozens of people. Each one nodded at him as he made his way deeper into the cemetery.

One man tipped his hat, a woman smiled gently, and someone else bowed deeply.

As Horace walked the gravel path toward the Beeson Crypt at the back, he saw the now-recognizable figures of the young Dodge brothers.

John spoke. "You've done it, Horace. You found the treasury and you've discovered the prophecy. Now all that is left for you to do is to open a great gateway."

"A portal?" Horace asked.

"Not like the previous portals that you have discovered. Those took the Keepers to the past. This one will open up a connection to the future," answered John.

Horace Dodge now stepped forward. "You have read the lost prophecy, and now you are the one who must fulfill it."

He pointed out beyond Horace's shoulder. Horace turned around and saw the faces of the people in the graveyard. Standing at the front of the crowd was his grandfather. Horace began to cry.

"We are all here to support you on your mission, Horace. You are never alone." His grandfather pointed back toward the tomb.

Turning around, Horace watched as the Dodge brothers opened the doors of the Beeson Crypt. From where he stood, Horace could see the dark smooth surface of the Benben Stone as it sat on its altar.

A chill ran up his spine.

"The time has come. The stone must be returned whence it came," Horace Dodge proclaimed. "It is no longer safe here."

"But where is this portal?" asked Horace.

This time the answer came from his grandfather, who now stood directly behind him. "Detroit."

chapter twenty-three

Horace spent the rest of the weekend doing chores for his parents and trying to make sense of all he'd experienced over the last few weeks. The discovery of the destroyed portal at the farm, the new portal in the Stout car, the Benben Stone in the Beeson Crypt, and, of course, the recovery of the lost prophecy in Detroit. And he thought about the latest dream many times. What was his task? And who was the other Keeper in Niles? And how was he ever going to get to Detroit? He wished Herman had told him who the other Keeper was so he might have some help.

By Monday morning he was looking forward to talking

to his friends. But when Horace arrived at school, as soon as he stepped foot inside, Mr. Witherspoon, the principal, stopped him.

"Horace, can I speak with you for a few minutes?" A class of first-graders was walking down the hall toward the gym. "In private."

Like a punctured tire, his breath literally hissed as it rushed out of Horace's mouth. Talking to the principal was never a good thing.

"It will only take a few minutes. I'm sure Mr. Petrie won't mind." Mr. Witherspoon led Horace past the library and into the main office. Then he opened the door into his own separate office.

"Here, make yourself comfortable." Mr. Witherspoon pulled forward an oversize leather chair opposite his desk.

Horace sat down and looked around. Not much had changed in Mr. Witherspoon's office since Horace's first visit. It looked like the same books and papers were on the desk, and the same pictures still covered the walls. He imagined that the office probably hadn't changed in thirty years, or however long Mr. Witherspoon had been principal at the school.

After Horace had made himself comfortable, Mr. Witherspoon closed the door and then seated himself behind his desk. "It is best we have some privacy," he said. "Your mom called me earlier this morning and told me everything that is going on. She asked if I could keep an eye on you. I can only imagine how hard it must be to have lost your grandfather and now to hear the news about your grandmother." Mr. Witherspoon reached into a candy jar sitting on the corner of his desk. "Here, take one of these. Maybe it will make you feel a little better."

"Thanks." Horace unwrapped the plastic wrapper and popped the minty candy into his mouth. It actually did make him feel a little better, clearing his thoughts. Horace looked up. "My mom called this morning?"

"Yes." Mr. Witherspoon nodded.

"Is it about my grandmother? Is she okay?"

Mr. Witherspoon nodded again and then shook his head. "Yes, yes, yes. Oh, I'm so sorry. No, that is not why I asked you here." He turned around and picked up one of the picture frames off the bookshelf behind him.

"Actually, *this* is why I brought you down here."

He reached over the desk and handed Horace the frame.

Horace recognized the old black-and-white photo from his first visit to the principal's office. The picture was of three men; two he recognized as younger versions of Mr. Witherspoon and his grandfather. "That is very nice," he said, setting the frame down on the desk. He was trying to be polite. Mr. Witherspoon had already shared the photo on the day Horace had gotten the news of his grandfather's death. He hadn't noticed before, but the young version of his grandfather bore a striking resemblance to Horace himself, even his hair, which was sticking straight up.

Mr. Witherspoon spoke. "Why don't you look again, Horace? I'm not sure you saw everything."

Horace was growing frustrated. He didn't want to sit there and play games with the school principal.

Out of politeness, he picked the photo back up and took a closer look.

"Who do you see, Horace?" Mr. Witherspoon insisted.

Horace was tempted to roll his eyes. "I see you and my

grandfather as young men."

"No, you aren't looking hard enough." Mr. Witherspoon urged.

Horace stared down at the photo for another minute. There was nothing that special about it. Three guys standing in front of a building, getting their photo taken. Mr. Witherspoon was acting like this was the most valuable picture in the world.

"I'm sorry, but I don't see anything."

Mr. Witherspoon pointed at the photo again. "*Who* do you see?"

Horace was now irritated. "I see you. I see my grandfather. And I see . . ." His words trailed off as Horace looked closer at the third figure. It was hard to be certain, without the extra weight or the wrinkles. But as he squinted, Horace suddenly realized who the third person was. In shock, he dropped the picture frame on the desk.

He stared at Mr. Witherspoon.

Mr. Witherspoon was now nodding in acknowledgment from his chair. "Now you see."

"Wait, but how . . ." Horace paused and rephrased his

question into a statement. "It's Herman!" he said point-blank.

Mr. Witherspoon said, "Yes, it's him." He laughed before continuing. "Hard to recognize him in his younger years. He has seen a little wear since that photo was taken."

"But how do you know him?" Horace asked.

Mr. Witherspoon's face wore a large grin that ran from ear to ear. "Let me show you." Mr. Witherspoon now was rummaging through his desk. Horace sat there quietly, wondering if the man was about to pull out an old school yearbook. But then, after a few moments, Mr. Witherspoon raised his hand, holding up an object far more valuable or familiar than anything Horace would have expected to see in a principal's desk drawer. The man placed a golden scarab beetle on top of the desk. Suddenly the desk was bathed in a brilliant yellow light.

Horace's jaw dropped, but then, before he could say anything, Mr. Witherspoon continued. "It has been a while since I've used this old friend to travel through a portal, but I keep it close just in case." He smiled. "Go ahead. You can look." He pushed the beetle over to Horace.

Horace flipped it in his hand. It was authentic, a scarab beetle just like his. He looked up. "Then *you* are the other Keeper! You are one of the other Time Keepers here in Niles!"

Mr. Witherspoon nodded. "Now, we mustn't keep that out too long, in case someone comes in." He reached out and took the beetle from Horace's hand. "But yes, I am he," he answered.

"But why didn't you ever say anything? Why didn't you tell me? Why didn't Herman or my grandfather tell me?"

Mr. Witherspoon ran his fingers over the smooth surface of the beetle, and its light flickered. "We didn't think it was safe. And, quite frankly, we didn't think you would need to know so soon." He looked Horace directly in the eyes. "Your grandfather was a great man, but none of us expected what Mr. Franken would do, or the dangers the Order would face. Your grandfather asked me to keep an eye out for you, but he also wanted you to discover the secrets of the Order on your own."

Horace shrugged. "Like the Benben Stone and the treasury?"

Mr. Witherspoon nodded. "Yes. When I was younger, learning the secrets of the Order was a great adventure for me. But I'm old, Horace. I can't go running through portals anymore. It's your time, your adventure, and your destiny to fulfill. Herman did not want me to reveal my identity to you at the beginning. We felt it was best to keep my connection to the Keepers a secret. But things have changed so quickly, and we have decided you needed to know."

"Mr. Witherspoon, can I ask you one question?"

"Yes, what is it, Horace?"

"Why does my beetle sometimes turn green? I thought it was always blue."

Mr. Witherspoon paused, and then scratched his chin. "There was only one other Time Keeper I know of who had a green beetle, Horace, and it was your grandfather. All I can think of is that when you brought your beetle near something that once belonged to your grandfather, like the sun has the power to illuminate an old fingerprint on a piece of glass, your grandfather's magic came back to life in the presence of your beetle."

Chapter Twenty-Three

"Wow," said Horace.

"Yes, it's pretty amazing." Mr. Witherspoon grinned. "There is a piece of his life force that lives inside of you."

Horace smiled to himself. The beetle continued to amaze him by revealing how deeply he really was connected to his grandfather, even after his death.

"Now, you'd better get to class. Keep working hard, and great things await you, Horace." Mr. Witherspoon looked intensely at Horace. "And one more thing."

"Yes?" said Horace as he stood up and moved to the doorway.

"I think you'll be happy to know that the sixth grade will be taking a class field trip very soon."

"Oh yeah? Where?" asked Horace.

Mr. Witherspoon smiled again. "Detroit."

a note from the author

In writing *The Search for the Lost Prophecy*, I found myself drawn back to my hometown of Detroit, a city steeped in a long history of secret societies, adventurous entrepreneurs, and mysterious connections to Ancient Egypt.

In the 1920s, Detroit was the fourth-largest city in America. From European immigrants to the Great Migration, hundreds of thousands of people descended on the city during the first half of the twentieth century with the hopes of capturing a piece of the American Dream. Two young inventors from Niles, Michigan, were Horace and John Dodge. Horace and his brother, John, became hugely successful in the auto industry, first working for Henry Ford and then forming their own car company in 1914. And while they didn't design the Stout Scarab, the car was in many ways a legacy of their commitment to innovation and cutting-edge design. Only nine of these bizarre beetle-shaped automobiles were ever created.

The Scarab Club was and still is a real organization located in the heart of Detroit and dedicated to the preservation of the arts. Originally founded by Robert Hopkins, the society was renamed in 1926 when it settled into its new home on the corner of John R and Farnsworth Streets. It's a small, unassuming building hidden behind the Detroit Institute of Arts. The second floor has an amazing wood-paneled study with a beautiful mural on one wall, the names of its past members written across the ceiling beams in chalk, and a stone fireplace with a scarab beetle carved into the capstone of the hearth.

Lastly, any visitor who travels to Detroit must also take a trip up Woodward Avenue and visit Woodlawn Cemetery. At the northern edge of the city, this graveyard, like Silverbrook Cemetery in Niles, is where the city's most famous residents are buried. At the back, resting among the trees, is a tomb of grand proportions. When I saw the emblem of Ra over the doorway, the two sphinx guardians lining the steps, and the Dodge name written across the doorway, I knew I had to tell their story.

est.   1907

acknowledgments

It takes a great team to write a great story, and I can honestly say that this was especially true when my little one entered the world in the middle of the writing process. With that in mind I'd like to thank the whole Sleeping Bear family, who were incredibly supportive and patient along the journey, even when I might have missed a deadline or two. I'd like to express my deep gratitude to Barb for her humor and insight; Catherine for bringing the story back into focus when it lost its way; and Jennifer for her design expertise. I'd also like to thank my agent, Clelia, for her inspiration and encouragement. And also my wife, Lauren, for caring for our little one those fall weekends when I slipped away to write. I know it wasn't easy, but thank you for your love and motivation. Last but not least, I'd like to thank Liam for whom this book is dedicated. Horace may have his beetle, but I'm lucky enough to have your bright smile. Thank you.

about the author

William (Bill) Meyer is an author, a teacher, and a student of history. He was born in Detroit and lives with his wife and son in New York, where he is finishing his PhD at New York University. He continues to teach his high-school students about the mysteries of Ancient Egypt, and share his love for his hometown of Detroit.